She looked at him, so much pain in her eyes—pain Andy couldn't understand—but still he felt it.

He tried to ask, to get Sam to talk, explain, but found he couldn't speak. Words weren't enough.

He brushed his lips across hers, murmuring her name, aware this might be a very wrong response, yet feeling her take something from it—feeling passion, heat and some unable-to-be-spoken agony as she kissed him back.

Somewhere in his head a voice was yelling warnings, but his body felt her urgency and responded to it.

The kiss deepened, her hands now on his back, tugging at his shirt so she was touching his skin—cold hands, cold fingers digging into his skin, dragging him closer and closer. His hands exploring now, feeling the dip of her waist, the curve of her hips, moving lower to press her into him.

Dear Reader,

For many years, I have enjoyed visits to the regional city of Port Macquarie, on the midcoast of New South Wales. It has appeared, under different names, in a number of my books, and I always see it in my mind's eye as I write.

Twelve months ago, I was fortunate enough to be taken on a tour of the new hospital there, and the first seed of an idea for a book was planted.

A chance meeting with an intensive care specialist made me realize just how much training goes into producing these vital members of the hospital community—six years on top of their six years of medical training, then a further year for pediatric intensive care here in Australia.

And that's how, for me anyway, a story is born—two random things coming together. All I had to do was add a hero and heroine and it was done.

For some reason, the idea of a friends-to-lovers story was niggling in my mind, and it seemed a while since I'd used that scenario. So I let it take shape, added characters, and the story was born.

Meredith Webber

ONE NIGHT TO FOREVER FAMILY

———

MEREDITH WEBBER

HARLEQUIN
MEDICAL
ROMANCE

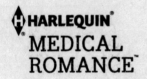

HARLEQUIN®
MEDICAL
ROMANCE™

Recycling programs
for this product may
not exist in your area.

ISBN-13: 978-1-335-14971-8

One Night to Forever Family

Harlequin Enterprises ULC
22 Adelaide St. West, 40th Floor
Toronto, Ontario M5H 4E3, Canada
www.Harlequin.com

Printed in U.S.A.

Meredith Webber lives on the sunny Gold Coast in Queensland, Australia, but takes regular trips west into the Outback, fossicking for gold or opal. These breaks in the beautiful and sometimes cruel red earth country provide her with an escape from the writing desk and a chance for her mind to roam free—not to mention getting some much needed exercise. They also supply the kernels of so many stories that it's hard for her to stop writing!

Books by Meredith Webber

Harlequin Medical Romance

Bondi Bay Heroes
Healed by Her Army Doc

The Halliday Family
A Forever Family for the Army Doc
Engaged to the Doctor Sheikh
A Miracle for the Baby Doctor
From Bachelor to Daddy

New Year Wedding for the Crown Prince
A Wife for the Surgeon Sheikh
The Doctors' Christmas Reunion
Conveniently Wed in Paradise

Visit the Author Profile page
at Harlequin.com for more titles.

CHAPTER ONE

SAM REILLY KNEW she shouldn't be walking into a large hospital with a well-travelled and probably germ-laden backpack towering over her, the soft roll of the sleeping bag on the top pushing her head forward so she probably resembled a bedraggled turtle as she made her way towards the reception desk.

She leant against the counter, easing the weight on her back slightly.

'I know I don't look much,' she said to the polite woman on the other side of the desk, 'but the road out from where I was working was washed away in a typhoon and it's taken me a month to get here. I need a shower, some scrubs, and if possible a white coat so that I can present myself as a reasonably competent doctor up in the PICU. My name's Sam Reilly—well, Samantha, really, but people call me Sam.'

'*You're* the new PICU doctor? I was told to expect you but, oh, my dear, you can't possibly go up there looking like that! Think of the germs you're probably carrying.'

'Exactly!' Sam said, 'Which is why I need that shower and something clean to wear. Can you help me out?'

The woman eyed her doubtfully.

'I guess you'd be okay in the ED staffroom. There are always plenty of clean sets of scrubs in there—showers, too, of course. Just continue down this passage and you'll find it on the left.' The woman hesitated. 'It's often a bit messy,' she added, as if a scrawny, redheaded backpacker might not have understood messy...

'And I'm not?' Sam queried with a smile.

Apart from a youngish man, sleeping like the dead on a most uncomfortable-looking couch, the staffroom was empty—but it *was* only six in the morning and he'd probably been on duty all night.

The showers were easy to find, but the cubicles were small, so Sam set her backpack down in the adjoining changing room, removed the sleeping bag—why on earth had she not thrown it away?—and dug into her pack for the meagre selection of new clothes she'd bought at Bangkok airport.

Four bras, four pairs of knickers, three pairs of socks and a new pair of sneakers, which had cost more than double all her other purchases put together. She found her toiletries, too, deodorant, toothpaste and brush, a wide-toothed comb that could handle her unruly locks, and a couple of strong hair clips she hoped could hold those locks in place.

Next, she removed a plastic-wrapped bundle and took out her stethoscope, watch and tiny torch.

A cupboard on one side of the changing room yielded sets of scrubs stacked under small, medium and large labels. Sam selected a large, which would swim on her small frame but experience told her she needed them for her height, though she'd also need something to use as a belt to hold up the trousers.

And finally, leaving everything she wanted to wear on the small bench in the cubicle, she stripped off and stepped under the water, cold at first but then so deliciously warm she could have stayed there for hours.

Unfortunately, the time she'd spent with her mother in the small hospital near the

Thai-Cambodian border—three weeks that had become seven when the typhoon had taken out the access road—had taught her the importance of clean water. She used soap from the dispenser on the wall to wash her hair and then the rest of her body, sluicing away the stiffness of thirty hours', mostly uncomfortable, travel, and whatever foreign microbes she might have been carrying.

Once clean she roughly towelled her hair as dry as she could get it, used another towel on her body, then dressed in new underwear and the scrub suit—way too big but still better than a medium that would have her ankles and wrists sticking out.

She dragged the comb through her hair, taming it sufficiently to pull it up onto the top of her head and secure it with a couple of clips. Somewhere there'd be a supply of bandanas—one to cover her hair and another she could possibly use as a belt—but in the meantime, with a white coat purloined from the cupboard—she felt presentable enough to find a café or canteen and have breakfast before fronting up for work.

In the outer passage, she found a row of lockers and spotted an empty one with a key in the door. She dumped her gear into it, locked it and pocketed the key. Now to find the canteen and some much-needed food.

Excitement at being back at work and back at home—back where she belonged, even if *was* a new hospital in a new city—made her want to skip along the corridor, but hunger was gnawing at her stomach. She'd been travelling for hours and she knew she had to eat before starting work as a senior PICU physician.

Andy looked up from the meal he was eating, unsure whether it was dinner or breakfast—just that he'd needed it after a more than hectic night on call for the PICU. The little boy with the burns to the soles of his feet had reacted badly to the pain relief they'd given him in the Emergency Department and had had to be stabilised before they could turn their attention to his injuries.

Redheaded little boy…

Andy smiled to himself. He'd once heard a statistic about children with self-inflicted burns that suggested nearly all of them were redheaded boys, and since he'd heard it he'd been surprised by how often it had turned out to be true.

Just then, he noticed another redhead who

entered the canteen. She was anything but a boy, and he felt an all-too-familiar jolt in his chest.

He'd known she was coming, of course—how could he not? As head of the PICU he'd read her résumé and been present at her interview. But the interview itself had been by a very static-filled radio link-up to some obscure place on the Thai border with Cambodia, and he hadn't seen her.

Not physically at least.

But in his mind's eye, she'd been as clear as day—a tall, redheaded woman who strode through life towards whatever it could throw at her, prepared to meet and beat any challenge.

Except that the last time he'd seen her she'd been in a hospital bed, the scattering of freckles across her nose and cheeks standing out against sheet-white skin, fury flashing in her pale green eyes as she'd told him to get out and never come back...

'Now!' she'd added in a strangled voice, and he'd left—walked away, his heart heavy with the loss of his best friend and aching for the woman on the bed who had looked so lost and vulnerable. Sorrow, anger and grief had churned inside him—fear for her, too—and words he should never have said had come out of his mouth. But now his head had told him just how stupid he had been, virtually accusing her of Nick's death, adding to her pain, while his heart?

Who knew where his heart had been back then…?

Life had thrown plenty at her since then, yet here she was—shoulders back, head held high, walking into the place as if she owned it.

Hiding the butterflies in her stomach— surely she'd worked in enough places to no longer have that uneasy feeling when she entered somewhere new—Sam crossed the canteen towards the self-serve shelves. She slotted onto the end of a small queue of people either coming off duty and needing food because they'd been too busy to eat all night or going on duty but needing sustenance before they tackled a new day.

She grabbed a packet of sandwiches and a bottle of some greeny-yellow juice and headed for the checkout, suddenly aware of a prickly feeling on her skin, as though someone was watching her.

She glanced around at what appeared to be a typical crowd in any hospital canteen at change of shifts, with subdued conversation and exhaustion leaking into the air. Sam paid her bill and headed for an empty table she'd spotted on the far side of the room. She had an hour before she was due to report to the head of department, but she'd eat then go on up to the ward, explain who she was and familiarise herself with the place—once she'd found a belt.

'You've gone all out to impress your new colleagues in that outfit,' a voice said above her head, and as her heart registered just who the voice belonged to, Andy Wilkie lowered his tall, solid frame into the chair opposite her.

'Andy?'

Damn her voice! The word came out as a pathetic squeak!

'What are you doing here?'

Much better—practically a demand...

'Did you not do *any* research on the place before you applied for a job?'

Andy's expressive eyebrows lifted above blue, blue eyes.

Sardonically?

Damn the man!

'I saw the ad online in an internet café in Bangkok. I'd just got off a flight from London and knew my stay with Mum would only be a few weeks, so I shot off an application and résumé while I was there. But I didn't have time to look into either the hospital or the staffing side of things.'

She hoped she sounded more composed than she felt, because the realisation that she'd be working with Andy had caused panic and despair to swell inside her.

The same Andy who'd blamed her for his best friend's death...

Which she probably had been...

But that was her guilt to cope with, her memories to haunt her, and right now she had to make some rational explanation about why this had come as a total shock. This was the start of a whole new life for her—she had to put the past behind her and start afresh.

She slammed the door closed on those painful memories, and remembered instead the good times when she, Nick and Andy had been friends—good friends who had laughed together. Although she'd seen less of Andy after she'd married Nick...

But right now she had to explain. Preferably without sounding as if she was making excuses.

'I was spending a few weeks working in a

small hospital—more a clinic, really—near the Thai border with Cambodia when the phone interview was set up. Actually, the interview on my side was mostly static. Were you one of the voices on the phone?'

'Of course!' he replied, no glimmer of expression on his face. 'I am, after all, the department head.'

Her boss!

Andy had employed her in spite of what had happened between them in the past?

'But *you* must have known it was me. After all, you had my application and résumé,' she said, trying to ease the tension in her body, praying it wasn't revealed in her voice. 'You gave me the job.'

He half smiled, and while her heart skipped a beat at the sign of this softening on his part, his voice was still cool and unemotional as he said, 'You were by far the best applicant. Anyone who's done eighteen months in the PICU in the biggest children's hospital in London has had more experience than all the other applicants put together.'

Sam closed her eyes, just briefly, stilling the confusion inside her.

She could do this.

She could work with Andy.

Actually, she doubted there were many better than Andy to work with. He'd headed east to America after Nick's death, while she'd fled west, first to Perth on the other side of the country and then London—the other side of the world—before spending three weeks that had grown to nearly seven with her mother in the tiny medical outpost on the Thai-Cambodian border.

Of course she could do it!

Play it cool!

'I'm sorry about the scrubs, but we had a typhoon a month ago just when I was due to leave, and the road to the nearest town was washed away. I finally got out, and onto a flight from Bangkok last night, changed flights in Sydney, and came straight from the local airport.'

'With no clothes?'

He sounded so disbelieving she had to smile.

'I could hardly take my winter clothes to Thailand, but I did buy some new undies at the airport in Bangkok,' she assured him, 'and as today was to be an orientation day, I'm hoping I'll have some time later to get out and buy something new. I'll need to book into a hotel, too, until I find somewhere to stay.'

He shook his head—disbelief at her story clear in his eyes.

'I'd have been here a month ago if it hadn't been for the typhoon. Plenty of time to have found things to wear and a place to live!' she said, cross with herself for the defensive justification.

'Well, eat up and we'll do the business side of things, and then I'll show you around the hospital. Just get some clothes, but don't bother with a hotel. I can give you a bed at my apartment for a night or two.'

He flung the words at her so casually—coolly—she didn't have a clue how to take them.

Simple politeness?

Or exasperation that she was so disorganised?

'You don't have to do that. I'll be fine in a hotel,' she told him, not adding that she'd also be far more comfortable away from him.

Staying with Andy? The very thought had tension tightening her nerves...

He studied her, eyes revealing nothing, although the words, when they came, were cold—their meaning clear.

'You *are* the widow of my best friend, of course you should stay with me, Sam.'

The best friend you think I killed, Sam thought as she drained the rest of her juice to help swallow the dry piece of sandwich.

But given that, could she really stay with him, even for a few days while she found somewhere else to live?

Although the offer might just be a peace offering. And it wasn't going to be for ever, she might have found somewhere else to stay by tomorrow...

And they *had* been friends.

And just what were you thinking? Andy asked himself. Inviting her to stay like that?

Especially as just seeing her again had stirred up so much consternation in his gut.

Even in baggy scrubs and her wet hair bunched somehow on the top of her head, she was still one of the most attractive women he'd ever met.

But she'd ended up with Nick—and, as far as Nick was concerned, she'd belonged to him. But could a woman as strong-willed and determined as Sam ever *belong* to any-one? Nick had certainly thought so, and somehow she'd made their marriage work.

Though, knowing Nick, that wouldn't have been easy…

Why was he thinking of the past when it was the immediate future he needed to solve?

It could be weeks before she found a place, months even, because the summer holiday season was approaching fast and accommodation owners made more money with short-term holiday rentals at this time of the year.

So why the hell had he suggested she stay with him, even for a couple of nights?

Exhaustion was the answer. He'd been operating the department without a first-class number two for nearly six months, the previous incumbent having left in a huff for not getting the top job. Others had filled in, of course, but none of them had wanted to take on too much responsibility for a job they'd never get.

But he'd asked her now and he had to live with her answer. Maybe she'd feel just as uncomfortable about the arrangement as he did and would find somewhere else really quickly.

But there was no time for conjecture, Sam was already on her feet, pushing back her chair, the far too big scrubs sliding down her legs to reveal a startling pair of lacy purple panties.

Scarlet with embarrassment, she grabbed the trousers and pulled them up, glaring at him as she muttered, 'There was very little choice of underwear at Bangkok airport!'

'Great colour!' he said, mainly to see her blush deepen. 'Pity you can't wear them on the outside like a superhero.'

She looked seriously at him and he guessed she was wondering how things would be between them, working together in the PICU.

'I'm no super-hero,' she said quietly. 'But I've learned a lot and can do my job.'

And having put him right back in his place, she offered a small smile before adding, 'But right now I need a bit of string or something to hold up these trousers.'

She marched ahead of him out of the canteen, one hand holding the errant scrub trousers tightly to her waist.

He followed close behind her, his head still asking why the hell he'd done this—chosen her for the job when he'd known it would mean the pair of them working closely together.

Yes, she'd been the best candidate and he had no doubt she'd be superb, but that strong niggle of attraction—he'd always hesitated to call it more—he'd felt from the first moment he and Nick had laid eyes on her, in the staff's favourite bar across the road from their old hospital, had never really gone away.

He flinched with embarrassment as he remembered that night. He and Nick had done Rock, Paper, Scissors to see who'd ask her out and the rest, as the saying went, was history. Sam and Nick had been married within three months, and he'd managed to distance himself from the happy couple as much as possible. Nick had been his friend from childhood—no way could he be lusting after Nick's wife...

'Something to keep my trousers up,' that same woman reminded him, bringing him out of the past and back to the present—and to the decision that as Nick's widow Sam was even more unattainable.

'There'll be a bungy cord in the janitors' room—everyone needs bungy cords.'

He ducked in front of her to lead the way, but as he passed, he couldn't help wondering how *she* was feeling about this. She'd certainly been startled to see him, so obviously hadn't had time to learn much about the new hospital or its PICU staffing.

He opened a door on the right and rummaged around through miscellaneous junk, finally finding not a bungy cord but a ball of twine.

'Put your hands out from your sides while I measure how much we'll need,' he said, stepping behind her and unrolling the twine, wrapping it around her waist—not easy when one hand still held tightly to the trousers—until his fingers met at the front.

'Leave enough to tie a bow,' she said, grabbing at the other side of the trousers before they slid down again. 'I don't want to be cutting myself out of it later.'

He didn't answer—couldn't. This was Sam, right here in front of him, more or less in his arms...

He'd denied this attraction, even to himself, for the three long years she and Nick had been married. He'd avoided her—avoided seeing her with Nick—and now she was here, and her closeness filled his senses. The smell of her seemed to invade his whole body.

It was hard to deny his attraction now, when she was so close.

So why the hell had he asked her to stay with him?

And why had she agreed? Especially given

how much he must have hurt her with his accusation as she had lain in hospital…

Or had she agreed?

Not in as many words.

She just hadn't outright refused.

There'd surely be a hotel available—could he find her one?

Or would that look churlish?

Yep!

And it wasn't as if he'd asked her to live with him, He'd just offered her a bed until she found something else.

Soon, he hoped…

He pulled back, away from her, the twine ball clutched in his hands. He had to get a life, find a diversion, take out a woman, any woman—anything to keep Sam out of his system.

He found a knife and cut the length, then handed it to her to tie it around her own waist, easing further away from her, his mind churning with the knowledge that she still had such an effect on him.

Sam tied the twine around her waist then turned the top of the trousers over it so the tunic hung neatly over them—more or less. Fiddling, fiddling, giving herself time to get over the startling discovery that Andy's arms around her—innocent as the movement had been—had brought heat to her cheeks and sent shivers down her spine.

Prolonged abstinence—that's all it was! In the three years since Nick's death she'd had only one relationship and although occasional sex had been involved in it, it had been more comfort than physical fulfilment that she'd wanted.

But Andy?

She'd met him and Nick together, and although it had been Nick who'd asked her out then courted her into a whirlwind marriage, she'd always liked Andy, had felt a kind of kinship with him. There'd always been something steady and reliable about Andy, though she'd seen less of him after her marriage.

Now he marched away after handing her the twine, and she had to hurry to catch up with him, falling in almost beside him, just a half-step back.

Deference to the boss, or fear that being closer might disturb her in some way?

Nonsense. It was simply because of the past that she was feeling uneasy...

He used a card to access what was obviously a staff elevator and punched the number for the fourth floor.

'You'll get one of these with your information pack,' he told her, 'and sometime today you'll need to have a photo taken to put on your ID—it only takes a few minutes.'

End of conversation, the elevator doors opened and they stepped into a corridor, Andy turning left and pushing through pneumatic doors.

They'd barely entered when a nurse appeared.

'Andy, they need someone down in the ED, eighteen-month-old with a temp of thirty-nine C, listless, flushed, unresponsive.'

'Come with me,' Andy said to Sam as he turned on his heel and headed back to the elevator.

'These two elevators are staff only. Well, they're used for moving patients as well, but the hospital is fairly new and the design is really brilliant, which makes working here a dream.'

He paused, then added, 'How often have you stood in an elevator and known there are at least three people in it who'd like to ask you a question about a patient?'

'And often did,' she added as she nodded her agreement.

This was good, this was work. She could not only handle working with Andy but she would enjoy it, aware that he was extremely good at what he did.

If she locked the past away where it belonged, treated Andy like any other colleague, and just concentrated on work...

He led the way into the ED, which was strangely quiet early in the morning, and a nurse hailed him as he walked in.

'We've put her in an isolation room—she's pink but that could just be the fever,' she explained.

'Or measles,' Andy ground out savagely.

He walked into the room and leant over the child, Sam slipping around to the other side of the bed, the small girl on it staring blankly at the ceiling. Her eyes were red, her nose oozing mucus, and flat red spots covered her forehead and were appearing as they watched, down her face and neck and onto her torso.

Speaking quietly to the child, Andy eased her mouth open and peered inside, finding tell-tale signs of measles in there as well.

'We need to check with her parents if she's

been vaccinated, although somehow I doubt it as the measles vaccine provides almost one hundred percent protection.

'What checks have you done so far?' he asked the nurse.

'We've removed her clothes and sponged her down, given her twenty milligrams of paracetamol, tried to get some water into her but she's so unresponsive I was afraid she'd choke.'

Andy nodded.

'We'll admit her, take her up to PICU and isolate her up there. We can use IV fluids and add ibuprofen six hourly via her drip.' He paused, drew a deep breath, then said, 'I'd better talk to the parents. Who brought her in?'

'The father, but he had to leave. Both parents are lawyers apparently, but I have a phone number for him.'

Sam followed, trying to thrust images of the sick child from her mind, wondering just how this had happened in this day and age of preventative measures. But as Andy used the card for the elevator, another thought struck her.

'You've just come off duty, haven't you? Why are you following up on this infant?'

'You've never worked a few hours after your shift ended?' he asked, and she shrugged because, of course, she, and probably thousands of other doctors, had.

'Thought not,' he said. 'But I've not just come off night shift—it's one of the few perks of the job that I don't do night shifts. I came in earlier and then again at about four to see a child on the ward who was having breathing problems.'

He smiled, and although it was a tired smile, it affected her, deep inside, in a way she certainly didn't want to think about.

Andy had been Nick's friend, and for all the irritations she might have felt in her marriage, the difficulties and disappointments, she still felt loyalty to Nick's memory, and somehow being attracted to his best friend was surely the ultimate disloyalty...

And, anyway, it was just a smile!

Andy had always had a nice smile.

They left the elevator, and Andy led her to the main monitoring desk, pointing out the way all the rooms could be monitored at once and introducing her to Karen, who was the head nurse on duty that morning.

She watched as his eyes scanned the monitors, and knew he'd been taking a mental note of every patient, even leaning over the desk and picking up a paper file to check on something he'd seen.

He explained the new admission to Karen, adding, 'Keep trying the number they have for the father in case the ED didn't get hold of him. Let him know where we are at and how to find us.'

A short discussion on their other patients, then Andy turned away, leading Sam along a corridor and returning to the conversation they'd been having.

'Actually, it was my last shift on call, and I'd worked my schedule so I could be here for your orientation before heading off this afternoon for a rest and to try to get my biorhythms back into sync.'

'I thought biorhythms had been totally debunked,' she said as the elevator doors slid open.

'Not totally and anyway it always seems to me that it's a better word to use because it's more than the physical side of yourself— well, myself anyway—that has to sort itself out after being on call, but the emotional and intellectual sides as well. I don't know about you, but I don't think well after a change of shifts—not until the sleep thing is sorted.'

'And the emotional side?' Sam asked as she followed him along the corridor.

'Oh, that's been totally stuffed for years,' he said. 'Unless you're involved with someone else who works ridiculous hours and often has to dash off at two in the morning for an emergency, a normal relationship is impossible.'

'Is there such a thing as a normal relationship?' she couldn't resist asking, thinking of the trials and anxiety she'd often felt in her marriage to Nick. But they'd reached the room where the little girl was already up from the ED and was being intubated by a nurse in full sterile covering, while Andy was looking intently at the chart he'd collected from the door.

With ninety-nine percent of his attention on the child in front of him, that tiny one percent had been caught by something in Sam's voice as she'd asked that question. The one about relationships...

Had her and Nick's marriage not been the one of connubial bliss he and everyone else had always thought it?

Nick had certainly painted it that way.

'We'll need to find out about her family,' he said, dragging that errant one percent back into place. 'Siblings, parents and grandparents, children she might mix with in day care or kindy.'

'I know most kindergartens won't accept unimmunised children. I'm not certain whether family day care is covered by it,' Sam told him, although he'd been speaking to the nurse.

'Her family—or at least one of them—should be with her,' the nurse muttered, but Andy ignored them both.

'There's a phone number for the father. When you speak to him just check out all you can about anyone she's been in contact with. If she has siblings who haven't been vaccinated, we need to get them in—or get them to their local doctor—for vaccination now. If she's been with other children at risk, we need to find them and get them vaccinated too.'

'Within seventy-two hours,' Sam finished for him. 'I could do that.'

He frowned at her.

'You're here for orientation,' he reminded her, a little too sharply because what he could only put down to lack of sleep was making him overly aware of Sam by his side. Reminding him he'd been foolish enough to ask her to stay with him at his apartment.

He stepped aside and wrote up the protocols for the day, handed the chart to the nurse, saying, 'I'd have liked to speak to a family member before admitting her, but I couldn't leave her in the ED. We'll have to explain that to someone later.'

He left the room, Sam on his heels.

'Why Intensive Care not the children's ward?' she asked, and he seized on the question to shake off the weirdness going on with this woman's reappearance in his life. Dear God, he'd known she was coming—had been looking forward to working with her again, given the experience she'd gained—and stupidest of all, he'd thought that long-ago attraction would surely have burnt out...

He banished the distracting thoughts, put them down to tiredness. This was work, a child's life was at stake.

'We can isolate her better here, watch for any signs of complication.'

'Pneumonia, encephalitis?'

'Ear infections,' he added, shaking his own head as if that might dislodge the softness of her voice.

Forcing his mind back to work, he led

her towards the nurses' station, situated in the centre of the ward where a team of five nurses monitored the live feeds from all the PICU beds while two clerical staff handled phones and paperwork.

'This is Dr Sam Reilly,' he said as several of them looked up. 'She starts here tomorrow and I'm showing her around.'

He waved Sam forward before adding, 'No point in introducing you all now, she'll meet you in time.'

He turned to one of the clerical workers.

'I've just admitted a three-year-old girl with measles and put her in Isolation Room Two. Could you chase up the electronic file from the ED and make sure the room's on-line for monitoring?'

'We use paper files that stay with the patient, as well as electronic,' he said to Sam as he whisked away, aware she was just a step behind him—aware, too, that he should slow, they should walk together, as colleagues did.

But although he'd been prepared for her arrival, even looked forward to seeing her again, having her on his team, the fact that her physical presence still perturbed him had thrown his mind into chaos.

It was only temporary, this reaction. They

hadn't parted on the best of terms—no, they'd parted on the worst of terms, he'd hurt her badly—so this would pass.

Soon, he hoped…

He thought back to that day in shame, but he'd seen her there in the hospital bed, so pale she'd have disappeared against the white pillow case if the scattering of freckles across her nose and the tangled red hair hadn't stood out so clearly.

She'd been injured, but just the sight of her—the pain he'd read on her face—had knotted something in his gut, something that he'd tried to burn away with anger.

And now?

Now she was a colleague, and he had to think of her that way, because that was surely the only way she thought of him, She'd certainly never given the slightest indication that she was interested in him—in anyone but Nick, in fact…

'Abby has encephalitis,' he said, forcing his mind back to work as he led Sam into another room.

The young girl in the bed opened her eyes and smiled wanly at them.

'We've no idea what brought it on, have we, Abs?' he added, coming closer to take

Abby's hand, 'but we do know she's on the mend.'

He motioned Sam forward.

'This is Sam, Abby, a new doctor and a very good one. We'll let her have a go at your records and see what she can sniff out, eh?'

Abby smiled again, then her eyes closed and she drifted back to sleep.

Andy handed the file he'd picked up from the back of the door to Sam, but kept his eyes on the sleeping girl.

Abby was thirteen, the same age Sarah had been when she'd died—Sarah, his beautiful, loving, always happy sister...

Sam flipped through the pages, noting the myriad tests that had been carried out on the sick child, realising that nothing had shown up as a possible trigger.

'Had she had a sore throat—could it have been as simple as a cold virus that triggered the swelling in her brain?' she asked as she slotted the file back in its place on the door, knowing she could read up on it on the computer later.

'Or some autoimmune thing, we've been thinking,' Andy replied, obviously still puzzled over the case. 'In fact, we did the regular tests, then stopped worrying what might have caused it and simply treated her. She's a little more alert every day, so I'm hopeful, given time and rest, she'll make a full recovery.'

'So much of what we do in PICU is rest and monitoring, isn't it?' Sam said, hoping she sounded rational and professional, although this being with Andy, trying to pretend he was nothing more than a colleague, was tying her stomach in knots.

And then he grinned at her.

'Ah, but the monitoring needs to be constant,' he said, while her head whirled. But Andy had always had that teasing grin so why…?

She dragged her mind back into gear and caught up with the conversation.

'Which is why the children are here and not down in the normal kids' wards. Come and meet Ryan—he's one of our frequent flyers.'

Sam laughed at the familiar phrase, reminding herself that this was work.

'Premmie?' she asked, and Andy nodded.

'He's two years old now, but still susceptible to any damn virus floating past in the air.'

'Usually RSV?' Sam asked, aware that respiratory syncytial virus, with its respiratory and breathing difficulties, was common in premature children.

Andy nodded.

'It's bronchiolitis this time. All the small passages in his lungs are inflamed, but six months ago it was pneumonia.'

'Poor kid,' Sam said, entering the room and peering down at the small form in the small cot. The little boy was probably only two thirds the size of a normal two-year-old, though what was really 'normal' with any child?

But she was intrigued by the small mask taped to the little boy's face and the tube from it leading back to a tiny CPAP machine.

'Non-invasive positive air pressure?' she said, intrigued why the usual nasal prongs weren't delivering oxygen to the little body.

'We're finding, particularly with smaller children, that it's easier to get them off the oxygen when we use the continuous pressure air pump. There've been various small trials on it, and no definitive data as yet, but it works for young Ryan here, so we stick to it.'

Aware there was no treatment apart from oxygen to help their battling lungs, fluid to keep them hydrated, and paracetamol to keep the child's temperature down, Sam followed Andy out the door. Studying him, thinking…

He would have had the final decision on her employment, yet he'd employed her anyway—even though he obviously blamed her for Nick's death.

She shut the box in her mind that held memories of that day. This was now a new life, and Andy would be, inevitably, a big part of it so sometime soon that box had to be opened and some of the contents discussed. Their last encounter especially needed some explanations and she knew they couldn't go forward with it in both their minds, blocking out any proper conversation or even, possibly, friendship.

But in the meantime, Andy was right here—her boss—and she had to prove herself to him.

He was tall—taller than Nick had been—and he carried himself well, except for stooping slightly to hide his height as he was wont to do. He was good looking, too, with his dark hair and blue eyes.

But not married—well, apparently not—there was no ring on his finger.

And why would you be checking that out? she asked herself. He doesn't even like you.

'We talked about monitoring earlier.'

The words brought her mind back to the job. It was probably a bit of jet lag that had it wandering so far and so fast.

'And though it seems such a simple thing, it's paramount. It means we can see when they're about to crash and need resuscitation, or stop breathing and need urgent intubation, or have a seizure and need protective care and medication to ease it.'

He frowned slightly, turning to look directly at her, before adding, 'Though why I'm justifying our work to someone who is as experienced as you I don't know!'

Blue eyes looked steadily into her wishy-washy green ones, and about a million synapses in her brain fired to chaotic life.

Breathe!

'You forget I've just come from a hospital that's barely more than a shed with some beds, and the most sophisticated medical machinery was an X-ray machine that we couldn't work because of a lack of electricity.'

Andy stared at her. 'Seriously?' he said, and she smiled, relaxing as she talked about the place she'd grown to love. A place where her mother, a nurse, had worked for so many years it had become her home.

'Well, we did have a generator and when we had fuel for it, and it actually decided to work for a while, we could get the occasional X-ray. Whoever had donated the X-ray machine to the clinic had included plenty of film, so from time to time it was very handy. Mind you, I wasn't there for long enough to get totally frustrated by the lack of technology, but it was very educational in its own way!'

Andy shook his head, and she followed him into the next room, where a very pale girl of about twelve, was lying listlessly on a bed. Her eyes were open but whether she was seeing them, Sam didn't know.

'Kayla has recently been diagnosed with Type One diabetes, but it took a while for her GP to get to the root of her problem.'

'Or for her to agree to even see a doctor,' Sam suggested, and saw the girl give a wan smile. 'A lot of girls going into the teenage years complain of being tired, of having headaches, or they're irritable. So it isn't always picked up on at home and they don't always get to a doctor until something drastic happens.'

'You're right, of course,' Andy agreed, and Sam was just deciding that this would be okay—this working with Andy—but then he smiled, and it was such an open, warm, typical Andy smile that something inside her began to crack.

Could it be the film of the ice she'd sheathed around her heart when Nick had died?

CHAPTER TWO

IT TOOK ANOTHER hour to visit the other patients in the ICU, including the little girl with measles who'd now been installed in an isolation room.

'Has someone been in touch with the family?' Andy asked the nurse who was checking the drip stand.

'The ED phoned the number the father left, but couldn't get him, but we'll keep trying. He could already have realised the implications and be taking his other children for vaccination.'

Sam nodded, hoping this was true, but Andy wasn't appeased.

'Come on,' he said brusquely. 'We're done here. I'll make sure one of the nurses gets on to someone in that family and tells them they need vaccinations urgently. It's probably best I don't talk to them when I'm tired and—'

'Angry?' Sam offered, and he shrugged.

'More frustrated,' he said slowly. 'You see a child so sick from a preventable disease and wonder what people are thinking of. Anyway, it's time I left. I'll take you back to my place, and you can do some shopping.'

Very frustrated, Sam realised, so she kept her mouth shut until he'd led her out of the hospital and into the car park, opening the door of a dark saloon.

The flashback hit her without warning— Nick's voice, loud and insistent, the car swerving. Then nothing...

She knew she couldn't get into the car; couldn't get in with an angry—or frustrated— driver.

Not again.

Not after the last time.

'I have to go back and get my things,' she said. 'My backpack. But you go. I think I'll stick to my initial plan and get a hotel for a couple of weeks until I find somewhere more permanent.'

The tightness she'd read on his face vanished like mist burnt off by the sun, and now anxiety drew its lines in his skin.

'Hey, it's okay,' he said. 'I just get a bit

upset when I butt up against parents like that.'

'Like what?' she retorted. 'A couple where both parents choose to work? Where neither wants to set aside the expensive training they've had, largely through public funds, to be with their children twenty-four seven? You don't know those people, Andy. For all you know, he could be representing a young girl in a rape case and can't afford *not* to be in court this morning, and the mother could be helping refugees in an offshore detention centre.'

He stared at her.

'You're saying they could both have legitimate reasons *not* to be with their child?'

'I am,' she said. 'I know there are parents who aren't totally involved in their children's lives, but we can't judge *all* working parents. Half the doctors at this hospital are working parents. Is a surgeon going to cancel a possibly life-saving op to sit with his sick child?'

Andy said nothing but she could see the idea taking root in his mind.

'So he'd focus on what had to be done—put his personal anxiety aside for as long as it took to get the best result for his patient—and then go back to the child.'

'Of course he would. Ninety percent of parents would.'

Andy studied her for what seemed like for ever.

'You've given this a lot of thought,' he finally said, and saw a deep sadness cloud her pale eyes.

But all she said was, 'Indeed I have,' before she turned and walked back towards the hospital.

He went after her, catching up in a few strides.

'Hey!'

He turned her so she faced towards him and used one finger to tilt her head so he could look into those tantalising eyes.

'Why don't you forget about a hotel for a while? Come and stay with me while you find somewhere permanent,' he said, hoping it didn't sound like a plea. 'It'll be fun—like the old days, although we probably won't see that much of each other because our shifts won't coincide, but…'

He paused and tried a smile.

'But when we *are* together, you can teach me not to judge, and remind me that every picture could be telling many different stories.'

She stood there, lips pursed—kissable, but he definitely wasn't going there—and he remembered she'd always done that when she was thinking.

When they'd all been friends.

'Okay!' she said, 'but I still need to get my backpack.'

He followed her back to the building, surprised when she led him into the ED staff lounge.

'I needed a shower before I ventured anywhere further into the hospital,' she explained, digging a key out of the pocket of her scrubs and leading him to a locker.

He watched as she unlocked the locker and reached in to haul out what seemed like an enormous backpack.

Sliding it out of her hands, he slung it over his shoulder, bending at the knees in faked collapse.

'It's not *that* heavy!' she told him, although he did win a smile.

Silly really, but the smile made the weight lighter, and he led the way back towards his car, feeling alive and alert, despite the early start. And if a tiny whisper suggested they should have parted when she'd suggested it earlier, he could easily ignore it.

It would be good to have Sam back in his life.

It *would*!

'It's not far from the hospital—my place,' Andy said, as Sam settled herself into the comfortable passenger seat in his car, 'but at night I like to use the car, the streets are dark and you never know who's hanging around.'

It was such an ordinary conversation Sam should have felt relaxed, but instead she was wondering why she hadn't insisted on going to a hotel. It wasn't that she didn't enjoy Andy's company—she always had, although she'd seen a lot less of him after she'd married Nick. He and Andy would meet up for a drink when she was on a late shift, or Andy would be busy when she and Nick were having friends over.

Then, so upset by what had been just his unthinking reaction to the accident, she'd refused to see him again while she'd been in hospital. But she'd been hurt by his angry words—hurt, if she was honest, because they had been too close to the truth.

But working with him meant they'd be colleagues, and colleagues were often friends, and she and Andy—

For heaven's sake, stop analysing everything. Whatever happened to your philosophy of taking each day as it came. That's what got you through the accident, and that's what you have to do here.

She glanced towards him, pleased he was concentrating on the road so she could study him for a moment. And wonder if perhaps she'd always felt a slight attraction towards him?

She shook her head.

'Bad thoughts?' he asked. He'd obviously seen her frown and head shake.

'No, just wondering where we are and how long it will take me to find my way around a new place.'

'You'd never been here before? Never had a holiday on the coast?'

She shook her head again.

'Mum worked full time—and I mean full time—two jobs usually, just to keep us fed and watered. Any extra money was put aside for the university education she insisted I had to have. Holidays never entered the picture.'

'Well, I'll just have to educate you. Port Fortesque was first settled way back, much of the original building done by convicts,' he explained. 'It was a stopping-off place for boats going north from Sydney to the new penal colony in Moreton Bay, which is now in Queensland but back then was part of New South Wales. There are still some lovely old buildings here, especially the lighthouse. We should go there for dinner tonight to welcome you back to Oz. They've turned the lighthouse-keeper's cottage into a fine restaurant.'

She'd let him talk, let his voice wash over her, although—

'I don't need fine dining,' she told him, 'and I definitely don't want you running around after me. You'll want a relaxing, early night after your four a.m. start, and I've got shopping to do and clothes to sort and wash.'

She paused, aware that what she was about to say was for her own protection. Andy was too darned attractive for his own good, and the less she saw of him outside working hours the better.

'I also need to get onto a real-estate website. There might even be a self-contained B&B I can use as a base until I get to know the area. In London, there were dozens of them set up close to hospitals.'

He glanced her way.

'Whatever suits you best,' he said, his

voice noticeably cooler. Surely he hadn't been *looking forward* to her staying with him. Wouldn't that put a crimp in his social life, for a start?

Although what did *she* know about his social life? Except that he'd be sure to have one. The Andy who'd been half of Nick and Andy had always had a beautiful woman in his life.

An image of Andy walking into his flat with a beautiful woman, chatting politely for a while before disappearing into his bedroom, had Sam feeling distinctly uncomfortable. Which was a totally ridiculous reaction as Andy's social life was none of her business, whether she was sharing his apartment or not.

Nothing to do with her.

At all!

He'd been—probably still would have been—her husband's best friend. She'd known him as long as she'd known Nick—which, much as she'd loved him, had, at times, seemed a very long three years—but Andy had always been there whenever he'd been needed, with a smile on his face and a ready laugh on his lips.

Except after the accident…

He'd been pointing out landmarks as they

passed, the river with its old wharf now only used to tie up visiting pleasure yachts, the surf beaches between rocky headlands to the south of the river mouth.

The sun sparkled on the ocean, making magic in the air, so when Andy turned into the drive that led to the basement of newish block of apartments, pressed a fob for the metal doors to rise, she began to regret accepting his offer.

It might be hard to leave the views this place must have, the rocky headlands curling protectively around the surf beach, a stretch of golden sand, the broken waves rushing up the beach as the tide came in.

'I thought you said it wasn't far from the hospital,' she said, as Andy expertly parked his car and came round to open her door.

She beat him to it, but only just, so she stood to find him so close they could have kissed.

If they hadn't been separated by the car door.

If this had been that kind of relationship.

And just where had *those* thoughts come from?

She might have felt a sudden awareness of Andy as a man, but she was probably the last woman in the world *he'd* consider getting involved with!

'I brought you the long way around to see some of the sights, but the hospital is only ten minutes directly west, twenty minutes on foot. Though I must warn you…' he added with a smile that raised goose-bumps on her skin.

What was wrong with her?

She tuned back into Andy's conversation.

'There are some steep hills to tackle if you're walking to work. This was once a rocky peninsula that reached out into the sea. There's actually good diving on it further out, colourful soft corals and tiny, brilliant fish darting in and out of it. Do you dive?'

'Dive?'

She invested the word with such disbelief Andy had to smile.

'You might not remember, but I come from a land-locked village in the top western corner of the state. We're lucky when we have a good enough wet season to have a swim in the local dam,' she told him. 'Plus, as you may have noticed, I have the kind of skin that turns beetroot red after about five minutes in the sun. The English climate really suited me!'

He did remember now—remembered more and more about her. She had two laughs, an infectious giggle and a full-blown laugh that was a sound of sheer delight.

And he'd asked her to stay with him?

He must have been out of his mind, especially when he loved to come home to the peace and quiet of his apartment after a busy day.

And now he was leaning on the top of the car door, talking about diving, of all things, and thinking about laughter from a time that seemed so far in the past it was practically ancient history.

Except that she was, and always would be, to him, quite lovely, with her vivid hair and pale skin, her easy smile and laughter.

Did he not want this light-hearted moment to end?

Or was he afraid that once she'd imprinted herself on his living space, he'd find it hard to reclaim it as his own?

His attraction to her had led him to distance himself from her and Nick after the wedding—not far, just far enough. Protection really, but she'd stayed in his head, usually laughing at some silly—

'Do you not want me to see your apartment, or have you sent an urgent message to some woman to vacate the place for a while?'

Her teasing smile plucked at his nerves, so it took him a moment to recover.

'Tribes of women having to vacate it,' he managed to say lightly, fully opening the car door for her and heading to the trunk to retrieve her backpack.

But the tension he felt as the elevator rose to the eleventh floor strengthened the feeling that maybe this hadn't been one of his better ideas.

Perhaps even his worst since the rock, paper, scissors fiasco all those years ago.

His mind did a quick mental scan of the state of his place. He liked it neat and tidy, but he'd left in a rush this morning. Although, while his bedroom might be a bit chaotic, she'd hardly be inspecting that. And this thought caused nearly as many strange reactions in his body as her pursed and kissable lips had earlier.

Enough!

This was Sam, his best friend's widow, remember, invited to stay while she sorted herself out.

A few days—a week—she was already talking about real-estate sites…

The problem was he'd known she was coming, but he'd been unprepared for actually seeing her again. *And* he'd been unprepared for the memories her presence had evoked.

He'd been attracted to her as far back as the day he and Nick had first met her, and he'd hoped she'd say no when Nick asked her out...

He'd telephone Susie later today, get his social life organised.

'Oh, but it's beautiful!'

Sam's words made him turn to see her gazing, wide-eyed, at his view.

'It takes in so much—the rocky headland, the sea, and then the sky. How lucky are you?'

He could hear the genuine delight in her voice, and for a moment wanted to tell her she could always stay on here, pay a little rent if it made her feel better. There was plenty of room...

Are you mad?

He hid more than a few qualms as he led her deeper into the apartment. This was not a good idea, given that he still felt a lingering attraction to her. Especially when, in his heart, he still blamed her for Nick's death, only too aware that never driving over the speed limit was a part of Nick's mild OCD.

In fact, the whole situation was a bloody mess.

'I like this room that looks back towards the mountains,' Sam was saying while he stood in the passage, clutching her backpack, random thoughts jostling in his head.

'Here, give me that.'

Her words broke the spell.

'I'll find something clean and relatively suitable to go shopping in and leave you to catch up on your sleep.'

He set her backpack down on the bedroom floor, aware of some new tension in the air. Had she guessed what he'd been thinking? Not that she needed to guess his thoughts about the accident—he'd more or less accused her of causing it.

'The bed's made up—friends and family are always turning up, so I leave it with clean sheets on,' he said awkwardly as he backed out of the room. 'I'll find some spare keys you can use.'

This was *not* a good idea, Sam decided when Andy had disappeared. They'd barely met again, and yet she felt unsettled when she

was with him. It was an awareness, really—
even an attraction—yet this was the man
who'd blamed her for Nick's death, probably still did...

Not that she had time to be worrying about
a little awkwardness, let alone attraction.
She'd lost a month of preparation back in
Cambodia and she had a lot of organising to
do. Clothes first—sensible clothes for work,
that's all she'd need for a while. A new swimming costume, there'd be days when she'd be
able to fit in a swim before work, before the
sun got too hot...

She opened her bag and rummaged
through it, finding some long loose trousers
and a tunic top—the kind of thing she'd been
wearing all the time at the little clinic. The
clothes might look a little odd in the shopping mall at Port Fortesque but they were
clean and decent.

Once showered and dressed, she found
Andy in the kitchen.

'We passed a shopping mall on the way
here. If I just go out the front door and turn
left, I'll find it, won't I?'

He smiled at her outfit—making her think
again of awkwardness and attraction, and

definitely finding a real-estate office on-line...

'They're clean and respectable,' she told him, defending her choice of clothing. 'The shopping mall?'

'Left and left again at the second street, you can't miss it,' he said, the smile still teasing at his lips. 'Phone me if you buy so much you need a lift home.'

He crossed to the bar on one side of the kitchen, undoubtedly used for most meals, and picked up a card and a set of keys.

'The fob opens the garage doors, the flat one you swipe for the elevator, the big key is for the front entrance and this lovely purple one is for my front door. Eleventh floor, Apartment Two. My number's on the card. Okay?'

She took them from him, their fingers tangling around the flat elevator key, sending such a weird sensation through Sam she involuntarily looked up to see if Andy had also felt it.

But although that teasing smile still hovered on his lips, he showed no sign of any sudden reaction.

Which was hardly surprising...

Sam departed, tucking the keys into her

small backpack, reminding herself that was something else she should buy—a handbag.

She shook her head. Her small backpack had served her well for the past three years. It had originally been Nick's, but he'd replaced it with a much smarter leather briefcase once he'd been promoted. She'd found it when she'd been cleaning out their flat and realised how handy it would be for her travels.

Besides, it was so long since she'd used a handbag she'd feel foolish with one, and she certainly wasn't going down the briefcase road. But she *did* have a small, pretty, handwoven bag with a long strap that would hold her wallet and a few tissues. She could always take that if she ever *did* go out at night.

The mall loomed in front of her, and she wondered just what it would offer in the way of clothes-buying options.

She needn't have worried, because all the old familiar stores were there, and within half an hour she had a selection of slacks, long shorts, skirts, T-shirts and shirts, and two swimming costumes. She'd stuck with basics—black and white with a few floral and striped tops to brighten things up— but as she walked out—newly bought shopping weighing down her arms—she passed a small boutique offering a fifty percent off sale.

The clothes were beautiful, mainly linen and silk, and simple in style but shrieking elegance. She tried to persuade herself that she'd never wear such clothes, but a pale green linen shift drew her like a magnet, while a black silk dress with a low scooped neckline and flaring skirt refused to be left behind. Sandals, shoes and a pair of comfy slides for the beach soon followed and she spent the walk home telling herself there'd surely be a Christmas party at the hospital so, depending on how formal it might be, either the shift or the black dress would do.

Back when she'd been growing up, buying her own clothes for the first time, her mother had always assured her that a little black dress could go anywhere. And her mother's LBD had gone many places—the single mother of a growing daughter not having had the money to spend on a range of 'going out' dresses!

'You didn't strike me a shopper,' Andy greeted her when she walked back in.

'I'm not,' she said. 'But having discarded all my London clothes before I left, and with the few Cambodian outfits not really suitable here, I had to start again. Basic shopping from the skin out, plus toiletries and odds and ends. I decided that being second in charge meant I had to at least look respectable.'

He smiled, eyes gleaming so she knew a tease was coming.

'Going to give me a fashion parade? You could start with the purple undies!'

She shook her head, but she was smiling too. This was the old Andy—often teasing her to see her blush, Nick laughing with him at the result.

Enough memories.

Be practical.

'You must be ready for an early night after your four a.m. start. As you've been good enough to take me in, would you like me to send out for a takeaway? Although I did grab a few groceries on the way home. I'd be happy to do a Cambodian stir-fry.'

'You cook?'

He sounded astounded.

In fact, so astounded Sam felt a little stab of pain. She'd always cooked and enjoyed it, but Nick had liked to give their friends the impression that she was a pampered princess, and he had always cooked the meals when they'd had guests.

She'd grown to hate it, but had kept quiet about it, at first putting it down to Nick showing off and only later realising it was part of his problem; his need to be the best in other people's eyes, both as a husband and a cook—even a doctor...

And she'd put up with it because she'd loved Nick, and she'd been determined to make their marriage work. Right up until the end—that last fateful day...

Focus!

'Well?' she demanded of Andy, possibly a little too abruptly.

He'd been frowning off into the distance, and turned, startled, back towards her.

'Well, what?'

'Would you like me to cook dinner?'

'Well, yes, of course,' he managed to say. 'If you really want to.'

'I do.' she said firmly, although she'd had to close her eyes for an instant to control a rising heat of anger.

So not only had Nick done his best to make *her* feel useless, but Andy's reaction had made her realise he'd convinced his friends of that as well.

The kitchen was neat and functional. No wok, but she could cook in a frying pan.

'Do you eat chicken?' she called to Andy, last seen standing on the balcony looking out to sea.

'Love it,' he said, sounding so close she started and spun around to find him on the other side of the breakfast bar.

'And you,' he asked, 'would you like a beer as you slave away over a hot stove?'

'Love one,' she said. 'You might not know it, but Cambodia has some very good beers, and one always goes down well while I'm cooking.'

He put the small stubby of beer in a foam holder beside the chopping board she was using to finely slice spring onions, bok choy, capsicum, carrots, snow peas and cabbage.

'Thanks,' she said, setting down her knife and lifting the beer. 'Cheers!' she said, and clinked it with Andy's.

'Welcome home!' he replied, smiling at her as if he meant it, and she had to turn away to hide the silly tears that had, for no good reason, filled her eyes.

Andy watched as Sam sliced and diced, taking a sip from her beer occasionally.

He'd thought he'd known this woman

who'd been married to his best friend for three years, yet small things were causing him to question all he'd known.

Not that it mattered. They'd be working and living—temporarily at least—together, plenty of time to get to know her. And if he was right about glimpsing a sheen of tears in her eyes when he'd said welcome home, then there was a lot about her to get to know.

He'd always admired her for the way she'd handled Nick, who hadn't always been the easiest of friends to have.

Nick had always wanted to win, to be the best.

Andy closed his eyes on memories and concentrated on the woman in his kitchen. Tall and lean in the loose-fitting, distinctly Asian outfit, she'd bunched her hair up on top of her head to keep it out of the way, and was humming to herself as she worked.

'You seem to enjoy cooking,' he said, watching as she opened a bottle of sesame oil she'd obviously bought earlier and poured a fine stream into the pan.

'Love it,' she said, echoing the words he'd said earlier, but turning to smile at him at the same time.

Tears—if they had been tears—now gone.

The pan sizzled as she slid the sliced chicken in and tossed it around so it would cook quickly. The vegetables followed, more sizzling, more tossing and turning.

She pulled her shopping bag towards her with her free hand, and half turned to him.

'I've cheated with the rice. Can you cut the top off the packet and microwave it for two minutes for me, please?'

He put down his beer and lifted the packet.

'Chilli and coconut, my favourite,' he said, as he did his part in the dinner preparation. 'I've come to regard microwave rice as one to the world's great inventions.'

She grinned at him, then added a variety of sauces to the stir-fry—small amounts but the aroma made the dish come alive.

'Right, rice into bowls, some eating utensils, and we're done,' she said, turning off the gas beneath the pan and raising her beer to her lips again.

Her eyes were shining, with pleasure now, he was sure, and as he watched the pale skin on her throat move as she swallowed the beer, a feeling in his gut told him this cohabitation might not be such a good idea.

But as they ate, sitting at the small table on the balcony, the moon silvering the sea, and the soft shushing of the waves the only noise, Andy found himself enjoying the company, the laughter Sam brought with the stories of her travels, and the allure of his beautiful companion, fine skin pale in the moonlight, stray strands of red-gold hair tumbling in long curls to her shoulders.

They talked of many things beyond her travels—the hospital, Andy's time in the US—but never Nick, for all he'd been an important part of both their lives. She thought Andy's conversation had swerved that way from time to time, but she'd turned the question or remark away, not yet ready to discuss this part of their past.

And aware she might never be able to...

Except she should—had to really—or it would fester and ruin any chance of a friendship between them.

She took a deep breath and launched right into it.

'That night at the hospital, Andy. I was upset when you said Nick would never have spee—'

'I should never have said it,' he interrupted. 'Never said anything so hurtful to you. Since we offered you the job, I've had this last month to think about how to apologise, trying to work out what—'

She reached out and touched his lips with one finger to stop his words.

'Me first,' she said, looking directly into his eyes, desperate to see understanding there, though at the moment there was only concern.

'I loved Nick to distraction,' she said quietly, 'but later I grew to hate our marriage. Not Nick—the love was still there always— but I hated what I'd let myself become, hated that I'd given so much of myself away to be what he wanted me to be, to fit into *his* life the way he wanted me to—the way *he* felt a wife should.'

She paused and looked down into her lap where her hands were tightly clasped, fingers twined into each other as she struggled with the emotion of those days.

'But that day—in the car—it suddenly got too much and the temper I was sure I'd conquered just erupted again, and I threw all the unkind and hurtful things I could find at him, at the man I loved...'

Another silence and she looked into Andy's face again.

It told her nothing, and a cold certainty

that she'd ruined any friendship they'd had and the one they might have had in the future spread through her.

But she had to finish.

'You were right,' she said, almost gabbling the words to get them said. 'I probably did cause the accident. I was as angry as I've ever been, yelling at him—him yelling back at me, both unwilling to give an inch. Then, suddenly it was over, a loud bang, and I was in hospital, Nick dead...'

She bowed her head, so he didn't see the tears—tears of pain for what else she'd lost that day.

'So you were spot on,' she finished, battling to keep her voice steady. 'Nick wouldn't have broken the speed limit, but he was as angry as I was, hurt and hurtful.'

She waited, praying silently that Andy would understand, wondering why life had to be so complicated.

But all he did was reach one hand across the table and squeeze her fingers.

Then he smiled, a weary, tired smile but one that still lit up his eyes.

'Oh, Sam, you shouldn't still be blaming yourself. I know I made things so much worse for you with my cruel, thoughtless words. And I've been wondering for a month how I could apologise to you. I had no right to say that to you—to hurt you further. Of course it wasn't your fault—you weren't driving, Nick was, and no matter the provocation *he* was the one speeding.'

He took both her hands in his now, and added, 'Can you forgive me? Can we be friends?'

She squeezed his fingers.

'Friends,' she said.

They sat a little longer, their hands still clasped, until Sam began to feel uncomfortable.

'You should be in bed,' she told him, needing to get away, to think about what had just happened between them, but first and foremost to remove her fingers, which seemed to be quite happy sitting there in his light clasp.

Andy had been trying to ignore their tangled fingers—ignore the tension rising in his body.

He stood up, probably a little too abruptly.

'I should, and so should you,' he said, clamping his lips together as beer and a single glass of wine had weakened his resistance, and the suggestion they could share a bed threatened to escape his lips.

As if, given how she'd just said she still loved Nick…

Or *had* still loved him?

He brought reality back with talk of work— safe talk.

'I did tell you, didn't I, that we'll be working together? Same shifts for the first few days, just until you settle in and get to know our routines and procedure protocols. Basic stuff, but I always found it difficult moving hospitals, so it seemed like a good idea.'

'That's great!' Sam said, a bright smile underlining the words. 'So, what time do we need to leave?'

Her enthusiasm *and* the smile made him wonder if it had been all *that* great an idea, but he battled on.

'We'll leave about seven-thirty,' he said, forcing the distraction of this beautiful woman away with practical words. 'See you then?'

CHAPTER THREE

'*SEE YOU THEN?*'

The words echoed in Sam's head as she made her way to her bedroom.

Did he not eat breakfast before he left for work?

And what was she supposed to do?

She remembered how she'd hated staying with a friend for the first time, never sure when to get out of bed—would everyone be up, or would she wake them?

And she'd certainly need breakfast but could she just open and shut cupboards in Andy's kitchen until she found breakfast-type food?

Not that she regretted him leaving so suddenly. Something had shifted between them after they'd talked about Nick. It was as if the breeze had strengthened in some way and caused vibrations in her body, a sense so fine she knew it had to be imagined.

Or hoped it had to be imagined…

Yet Andy's abrupt departure had eased that tension at least, although he'd left her wondering just what it was she felt.

Andy was just Andy—a friend from years back—and his having her to stay was nothing more than a sign of that.

But, practically, could they get back to the easy friendship they'd had when she'd first met him? From the way he'd spoken, he'd obviously regretted the harsh words he'd said to her after the accident, so she could put that behind her and go forward.

In friendship… Something, she realised now, she wouldn't like to lose.

She closed her bedroom door and was pulling off her T-shirt when there was a light tap from outside.

'I should have said there's plenty of food in the pantry and refrigerator, or there's a café on ground level that opens early to do breakfasts.'

She moved closer to the door, awareness of him just outside prickling her skin.

'Thanks,' she said. 'The café sounds good!'

She was close enough now to press her

hand against the wood, aware he was just as close on the other side.

Was his hand also against the door?

Did she want it to be?

Did *he* want it to be?

She waited, wondering if he'd suggest they eat breakfast in the café together.

Should *she* suggest it?

But all she heard was a shuffle of feet on carpet and a quiet, 'Goodnight!'

She stayed where she was, hand on the door, trying to disentangle the various emotions this nothing of a conversation had just stirred up in her.

Had she *wanted* him to come in?

She shook her head to that one, although she wasn't totally convinced.

Had *he* wanted her to ask him in?

Well, on that point she had no idea at all, but would guess not. Andy was far too… proper, really for something so crass…

They were going to work together—be colleagues—and relationships with colleagues grew muddled. She and Nick had discovered that.

Nick.

She'd thought three years would have made it easier to think about him—even talk about him—but the resentment and anger she'd begun to feel towards the end of their marriage had surfaced again when she'd started talking earlier. Perhaps it was best to leave things as they were…

She moved away from the door, stripped off her clothes and stepped under the shower in the little en suite bathroom.

But once in bed, a book propped on her knees, she wondered again about her agreement to stay with Andy—if only for a short time…

She did have breakfast in the café but ate alone—fruit toast and strong tea. No sign of Nick, no sound of him in the apartment before she'd left it.

But that was explained when she returned, and he was in the kitchen, mixing up some type of green sludge—presumably a healthy smoothie—a beach towel wrapped around his waist and his bare chest still damp in patches from an early morning swim.

She'd walk to work in future, she decided then and there. That way she wouldn't have to work out why that bare chest, tanned and sculpted by the swimming and whatever other exercise he did, had caused a hitch in her breathing, and a warmth to fill her body.

'I can walk to the hospital today,' she said, the words shooting out of her mouth. 'It'll do me good.'

He swallowed a mouthful of his green sludge and shook his head.

'I'll be five minutes,' he told her, 'I've had my shower, and—'

Dear Heaven, he was naked under that towel!

The warmth became heat, which she knew would be showing in her cheeks.

'No, I need the exercise, and it will be good to get a feel for the place.'

She grabbed the little backpack, checked the keys were in it, and with a casual wave of her hand escaped out the door.

What she really needed was a real-estate office or to start searching online for somewhere else to live.

No way could she continue to live with Andy now he'd started to affect her the way he did. Neither could she really find another man—just a friend with benefits—to ease her frustration, not while she was living with Andy. *That* would be far too awkward!

She needed to move out, find somewhere

of her own. Somewhere she could think about the future, put Nick behind her for ever, and, in the classic phrase, move on!

How had she got herself into this?

But as she walked up onto the top of the next hill and looked north this time, to the river's mouth and beyond it to the sweeping, golden beach and brilliant, dark blue ocean, a sense of peace stole over her.

Coming here *had been* a good decision.

And having a friend—for that was all Andy was—to show her around was also a good thing.

She walked on, breathing in the sea air, her feet beating out a rhythm that echoed in her head—Andy is a friend, Andy is a friend…

Rosa, the three-year-old with measles, was their first stop, after being alerted by a nurse that her condition hadn't improved.

'In fact, it's worsened,' Sam said as she read through the chart, while Andy bent over the cot.

'Yes,' he said. 'The night duty doctor phoned, and we discussed using the cooling pads.'

Sam had been looking at the small pads on Rosa's wrists, neck and temples, white against the raw redness of the rash that now covered her body.

'We're just getting new ones for the inside of her elbows,' the nurse explained, 'and her father's been here all night.'

She pointed to the big adjustable chair that could be tipped back to allow someone in it to at least doze.

'He's gone home to see his other children and take them to their local GP for vaccinations, then he'll be back.' She paused. 'He's devastated,' she said. 'Blames himself.'

Sam took one glance at Andy's face and stepped into the conversation.

'Some people genuinely believe the vaccination could harm their child. They fear it, no matter how much education we do.'

Andy shook his head. 'Were you always Little Miss Sunshine, refusing to see any bad in people?' he said, but it was more a tease than a sarcastic remark.

She grinned at him. 'I try,' she said.

They moved on to the boy with the burnt feet, Jonah. He was sleeping, and as Andy studied his chart, Sam looked at the bandages and shook her head.

'How on earth can you burn the bottom

of your feet?' she asked, and it was Andy's turn to smile.

'He lives near the beach and, apparently, he was clever enough to know he'd probably end up in serious trouble if he started a fire in the scrub on the headland. So he decided to experiment with a small one on a sandy patch hidden in amongst the rocks at the point. Had a great time, then his mother called him for dinner, and he covered it over with sand.'

'And walked on it?' Sam guessed.

'Worse,' Andy said. 'He stamped the sand down to make sure the fire was out.'

Sam shook her head. 'His poor parents,' she said. 'They must wonder what on earth he'll get up to next.'

They discussed his treatment—the worst of the wounds had been debrided, and both feet were now bound in bandages to prevent infection. Given his improvement, he could go into a general children's ward later that day.

Together they checked the most seriously ill children, three of them in isolation rooms following chemotherapy. Then Andy excused himself to attend a department heads' meeting, and Sam was left to visit the other children—twenty-three in all, quite a number for a provincial city's ICU.

'They come in from all the outlying areas,' the nurse with her explained. 'The district hospitals don't have the specialists or Intensive Care.'

'Certainly not as up to date as this place,' Sam said, constantly surprised by the facilities in the unit.

A loud beep took both of them to the small alcove where the child with RSV lay limply in his cot. One glance at the bedside monitor told Sam what was happening. His struggle to breathe, even with the ventilation, had caused his overworked heart to stop beating.

As the nurse pressed the button for a crash cart, Sam started chest compressions, the heel of her hand on the little breast bone, pressing hard and counting.

'Remove his mask for a minute and suction his trachea, in case the oxygen isn't getting through' she said to the nurse, as Andy, no doubt alerted to the crisis, appeared.

'His chest is rising and falling so the ventilator is keeping him oxygenated.'

Andy felt for a pulse, shook his head.

'Epinephrine?' Sam asked, and he shook his head again.

'There are so many questions about the use of it in the long term these days,' he said. 'It will probably restart his heart but could also cause brain damage. We'll shock him. You've got his weight?'

The nurse read it out from the chart and Sam watched as Andy translated it to voltage, using four joules per kilogram. The nurse was already attaching miniature pads to the small chest while Andy set the machine.

They stood clear and the little body jerked, Sam bending over him ready to begin chest compressions again, although the steady heart-rate lines were already running across the monitor.

It had been a heart-stopping moment—literally for the child—and the tension had somehow thickened the air in the room, while all eyes remained on the monitor, dreading they'd see that line waver.

Sam turned to practical matters, beginning compressions again, aware that continuing compressions for a couple of minutes helped the failing heart regain its normal momentum.

The nurses were cleaning up and wheeling the crash cart away, but Andy continued to study the boy.

'We need to go back in his history to see if there was any suggestion of an abnormality in his heart from birth.' He shook his head before answering his own question. 'Surely not. Premmies are always tested every which way, scanned and checked on an almost daily basis.'

Sam smiled to herself. Back when she'd first met Nick and Andy, and had worked with Andy when she'd been on a month's student placement and he a junior registrar, she'd often heard him debating his thoughts aloud.

'What about an atrial septum defect?' she suggested. 'They can sometimes be so small they're not picked up until adulthood, although they do affect the lungs as well as the heart.'

Andy smiled at her, which, given the situation, shouldn't have had the slightest effect on her, but when he added, 'I knew I'd got you here for a reason,' she felt a flush of pride.

'We'll let the little fellow rest for an hour,' he continued, while she told herself it really *was* pride, not something else that had caused the heat, 'then see what an ultrasound can find.'

'They're often picked up in adults with a murmur,' Sam said, concentrating on their small patient and sticking the buds of her stethoscope in her ears. 'If it was audible it would have been picked up before now, but I'll just have a listen in case the stoppage made it clearer.'

She blew on the pad to warm it, then pressed it gently to the little chest, hearing the beat of his heart, steady and regular now, and perhaps just a whisper of something else.

Andy listened too, but shook his head. 'We'll leave it for the ultrasound.'

He paused, thoughtful again. 'Although if it does show something up, we then have a decision to make—or the heart specialists will.'

'Operate to close it, or just leave it and watch?'

He nodded, frowning now at the child who'd had such a bad start to his life.

They checked the rest of their patients, including a large lad of twelve who looked out of place in the PICU.

'He took a knock on the football field, lost consciousness, then had a grand mal seizure,'

Andy explained. 'The neurologist who admitted him wanted him monitored for forty-eight hours before he does an EEG to see if there's a likelihood of recurrent seizures.'

He watched Sam flicking through the lad's chart, pleased he had such good support from his number two, even though working with Sam felt disorientating in some way. For so long she'd just been Nick's girl and that's the way he'd forced himself to think of her from the time they'd started going out together—Nick's girlfriend, Nick's partner, Nick's wife.

But Nick had been lost to both of them and now she was just Sam—a woman he'd been attracted to, and, he rather thought, still was...

And he'd been stupid enough to ask her to stay!

'His CT scan showed no visible damage,' she said, glancing up at him with a flash of pale green eyes. 'No bleeds or clots, no abnormalities that could have caused it, so it was likely the result of the concussion.'

He nodded, aware some response was needed, but—

You've got a patient! an inner voice said sternly, and he turned his full attention on the boy, asking him simple questions, noticing his patient's growing exasperation.

'And before you ask, I don't know who the prime minister is, and I didn't know it before either. It's a stupid question,' the lad said.

'So, tell me about your mates instead,' Andy suggested, and listened while the boy rattled off the names of his friends and gave them brief descriptions of each of them.

Andy smiled at him. 'I don't think there's much wrong with your brain, and the EEG— that's just short for electroencephalogram, which you must admit is a bit of a mouthful—will show if there's likely to be a recurrence, and you'll need to be on medication to stop it happening again.'

'But that would mean no more football,' the lad complained.

'No football for four weeks anyway,' he told the lad.

'Try tennis—it's much better for your head,' Sam suggested, but a little frown between her eyebrows made Andy wonder what was bothering her.

'Let's get a coffee,' he suggested as they left the boy to his video game. 'We'll talk about the children we've seen and you can tell me what you think.'

He led her into the small, comfortable staffroom and turned on the coffee machine.

'You okay?' he asked, carefully not looking at her but aware of her presence.

Aware of *her*...

Wondering if he'd made a mistake in appointing her when there was a close connection between them and he'd always been attracted to her.

Then reminding himself he couldn't have not employed her. She had been far and away the best candidate.

Wondering, also, why she hadn't answered.

It had been the kind of question that usually got a reply immediately.

So he had to turn, *had* to look at her, had to put up with the disturbances her presence was causing him, because she *was* the best and his patients deserved that.

'*Are* you okay?' he asked this time.

She smiled at him, but it was such a pathetic effort he forgot about the coffee, and his personal concerns, and sat down beside her on the couch.

'What is it?' he said, trying to sound gently persuasive but missing it by a mile.

Even to him the question sounded abrupt to the point of rudeness, but it had been the best he could do when every fibre in his being was telling him to put his arm around her—tell her that whatever it was they'd work it out.

Hold her...

Comfort her...

That might be what she needed right now, but was it what *he* wanted?

Forget that, think about her. It's what a friend would do—any friend.

But *were* they friends?

They'd certainly made peace between them...

She smiled again, a better effort, and added a half-laugh.

'Stupid, really,' she said. 'But I was looking at young Nathan and wondering if I could let my child play football.'

She studied him for a moment before adding, 'When you've got children—a family of your own—how do you make those decisions? Do they worry constantly, every parent, or is it worse for us because we see what *can* happen?'

He thought of the children he'd probably never have—the women who hadn't wanted to risk having a child with him—the scars that had made him stop thinking about a family, about any permanent relationship...

'I'm not sure,' he said, 'about other parents but I think it's probably easier not to have them, then you don't have to worry at all. That's where I've got to in my thinking.'

He knew it was a flippant answer but he didn't want to go into all of that with Sam when she was obviously upset.

Thrusting the confusion of thoughts out of his head, Andy returned to his coffee-making. But he *had* to think about Sam's questions because there'd been genuine concern in her voice, as if having a family was important to her and she'd need to know how to handle things.

Had she and Nick been arguing about that?

Nick certainly wouldn't have wanted a family—it would have diverted the attention from him. He chose instead to just answer her original question.

'About sport, that lad could just as easily have fallen out of a tree and hit his head or tripped at home. I guess most parents just do what they think is best at the time and hope their children survive childhood.'

She made a sound that could have been

agreement but continued to look pensive—
even worried.

He carried over a coffee, realising as he
placed it down in front of her that he hadn't
even asked how she took it, and wondering
why he'd remembered her coffee preferences
from the past.

'You remembered?' she said, looking up
at him, her eyes wide with surprise.

'It wasn't a hard choice to remember,' he
said. 'Black no sugar.'

He carried his own coffee over, along with
a tin of assorted biscuits.

'Like white, skimmed milk and half a tea-
spoon of sugar?'

She spoke lightly, but he heard a hint of
tension beneath the words and wondered, not
for the first time, how she'd ever managed to
live with Nick's little peculiarities.

She'd loved him to distraction, she'd said,
but had come to hate who she'd become in
fitting into his mould of her.

He understood that. He'd known Nick
nearly all his life and had accepted his pe-
dantic ways—for the most part—as simply
Nick being Nick.

But he'd been able to walk away; to find
someone else to play with, someone else to

discuss their studies with, when Nick had become too controlling.

Sam had not only loved the man, she'd been married to him. Hard to walk away from that.

Impossible, Andy guessed, to find someone else...

He watched as she dunked a biscuit in her coffee and sucked on the soggy end, drank some coffee, *then* looked across the table at him.

'You've probably read the latest studies on OCD, linking it to serotonin issues,' she said quietly. 'I tried to persuade Nick to try some anti-anxiety medication, which works for some people, but, as you know, he really couldn't see he had a problem.'

Which made Andy remember the accident, and his own personal conviction, at the time, that Nick would never have driven above the legal limit, could never speed—it was part of his make-up.

Perfectionism was how Nick had termed it.

So, now the fact they'd had an argument had been revealed, rather than solving things, it had made Andy more curious. It must have been about something really important, drastic even, for Nick to have reacted the way he had.

Had it been about them having a family?

Sam had finished her coffee. 'Back to work?' she asked.

'There's no rush. The staff know where we are. And we *did* come here to discuss the patients.'

He hesitated, wanting to ask how she was finding things but knowing it was far too early for such a question.

And, anyway, what he really wanted to know was more about her—about her life over the last three years—and how she felt about Nick now. Was she still mourning him?

Well, he wanted to know everything really.

Which was so unsettling a thought he stood up, collected her cup and the biscuits and made a business of washing the dishes, aware of her standing, moving towards the door—every nerve ending in his skin alive to her movement...

Weirdest coffee break she could remember, Sam thought, leaving her cup on the table because carrying it over to the taps would have meant getting close to Andy again.

She escaped from the comfortable room

to the routine movement on the ward but couldn't escape her thoughts. Thoughts that must have been written clearly on her face earlier because Andy had been so concerned—so caring—when he'd sat her down and asked if she was okay.

Which she really wasn't, considering it was so close to the anniversary…

But she'd welcomed the coffee break, sure they'd be discussing patients or talking about the hospital in general—even gossiping, which was the most common pursuit in staff-room coffee breaks. All of which would have got her mind off her own bleak thoughts.

But, no, somehow, without really speaking, they'd ended up discussing Nick.

And children—that had been the other topic, and a revealing one. Andy had spoken lightly but it sounded as if he'd, for some reason, already decided not to have children.

For a moment she wondered why, then realised all this was just another way to keep her mind off the upcoming date.

Work! That was a far better answer.

Her first stop was at the nurses' station to check that families of children who might have been in contact with young Rosa had been alerted by the hospital staff.

'Yes, we've got on to the private day care place she went to twice a week. Only five kids in all, and the woman who runs the place said she's spoken to all the parents, but we got names and telephone numbers and spoke to them again ourselves.'

The nurse—Damian, his name tag read—frowned. 'It's not the children I've been worried about but the old people,' he said.

'Old people?' Sam echoed, as she felt Andy materialise by her side.

'Yes. Rosa also went to a playgroup. The nanny took her one day each week. It was run in a nursing home. Apparently, the residents loved having the little ones running around.'

Sam closed her eyes, considering how quickly something like measles might spread through such a place.

'It might not be too bad,' Andy said, coming to stand beside her. 'A lot of older people have the measles vaccine when they're expecting their first grandchild. It's actually recommended by most GPs.'

'But would they all remember whether they've had it or not? And can we really vaccinate everyone in the place, given that many of them would have complex health problems?'

Sam had turned towards Andy as she spoke so read her own concern in his face.

'I'll get on to the people at Infections Diseases Control—talk to them,' he said. 'But I think it's going to be safer to vaccinate them all.'

'Is this really our problem?' another nurse asked, and Andy and Sam both turned back towards her.

'Who else's would it be?' Sam demanded. 'It's not as if we have to do the actual work, but we need to get authorities alerted to what's going on. And they, in turn, can make the decisions, even publicise the risk if they feel it's necessary.'

The nurse nodded, though she still seemed unconvinced.

'It's a very real risk,' Sam told her. 'A measles outbreak—even with a limited number of patients—almost inevitably results in some deaths.'

She turned away, disturbed by her own words, wanting to go back and check on Rosa.

And, if she was honest, wanting to put some space between herself and Andy, who'd been standing beside her for far too long. This awareness thing she was feeling would disrupt her work if she didn't get it under control. It wasn't as if Andy would ever be interested in her, given how he'd seen her role in the accident.

And hadn't he said that the reason he'd asked her to stay had been because she was the widow of his best friend?

Hardly a romantic invitation.

Rosa was still febrile. The drugs and cooling packs would be keeping her temperature below a really dangerous level, but she was still a very sick little girl.

Sam watched the monitors. Her heart rate was a little elevated but it would be, blood oxygen level fine, but it was being helped by the nasal cannula providing supplemental oxygen. A tube dripped fluid and drugs into her little body, but what else could they do?

She knew this was the problem with choosing to work with seriously ill children—some of them could not be saved. But deep inside she felt that wasn't good enough. They *all* deserved a chance at life—something her child had never had...

A nurse distracted her with a message about one of the chemo patients, and she was pleased to turn her attention from such dismal thoughts. She met the oncology consultant in the child's room, and from then on it seemed as if the world had conspired to keep her mind fully focussed on work.

Sometime in the early afternoon she grabbed a cup of tea and an apple in the staff-room and was looking forward to the end of the day when she could finally relax.

But Rosa's condition had worsened and neither she nor Andy felt happy about leaving the child. Andy made the excuse of paperwork while she stayed with the father in the room, bathing the little girl's body with a cool, damp cloth.

'She's not going to make it, is she?' the father asked at one stage, and Sam couldn't answer. He sat back in his chair and bent forward, elbows on knees, face bowed into his upturned hands, his despair seeping into the room.

Rosa died at four minutes past midnight in her father's arms, Sam standing with a protective arm around the man's shoulders, tears glistening in her eyes.

After a few minutes the duty doctor and

nurses moved in quietly, taking care of both the father and the formalities.

Andy slipped his arm around Sam's shoulders and led her firmly out to his car, aware of a terrible tension in her body.

But as he walked around to the driver's door, he looked up at the star-bright sky and wondered what the hell was going on. He'd understood Sam's desire to stay and care for Rosa, but when he'd forced her to leave the child for long enough to eat earlier in the evening he'd seen the tension in her body, and he'd had the sense of someone holding themselves together with only the greatest difficulty.

Now she sat, rigid in the seat beside him, her hands knotted in her lap, and instinct told him to get her home—unfamiliar though that home might be. She needed to be somewhere away from the hospital, somewhere he could put his arm around her shoulders when he asked her what was wrong.

But they only made it to the elevator of his apartment block before he saw the tears on her cheeks, so he held her as they rose, steered her gently into the apartment, and enfolded her against his body as soon as they were inside.

'Tell me,' he said quietly, sliding his fingers into her hair to tug her head back gently so he could see her face, flushed and tear-stained.

She looked at him, so much pain in her eyes—pain he couldn't understand—but still he felt it. He tried to ask, to get her to talk explain, but found he couldn't speak, words weren't enough.

He brushed his lips across hers, murmuring her name, aware this might be a very wrong response yet feeling her take something from it—feeling passion, heat, and some unable-to-be-spoken agony as she kissed him back.

Somewhere in his head a voice was yelling warnings, but his body felt her urgency and responded to it.

The kiss deepened, her hands now on his back, tugging at his shirt so she was touching his skin—cold hands, cold fingers digging into his skin, dragging him closer and closer. His hands exploring now, feeling the dip of her waist, the curve of her hips, moving lower to press her into him.

Then clothes were shed in an undignified scramble, Sam pushing his hands away and quickly peeling garments off herself.

They kissed again, and that magic moment of skin touching skin swept over Andy as he guided them both towards his bedroom, to the rumpled, unmade bed he'd had no time to straighten that morning.

In some dim recess of her brain Sam was aware this was madness—they had to go on living together—but right now, on the anniversary of her own baby's death, she needed the release—the oblivion—of sex.

So, as Andy's lips moved down her neck, as his hand grasped her breast, fingers teasing at the nipple, she groaned with the sheer, mindless pleasure of it, bit into his shoulder, and pressed her body hard against his.

They fell together onto the bed, mindlessly engrossed in pleasure—in pleasing each other and being pleased, teasing and being teased—until Sam could take no more and guided him into her body, revelling at how natural it was, moving in an age-old rhythm that eventually brought with it total release.

A long time later, it seemed, Sam woke to find Andy propped on his elbow, looking down at her, and as she watched, he reached out and wiped a tear from her cheek, holding it up for her inspection.

She rubbed her hands across her face, hoping to obliterate any more tell-tale signs there might be, then slid carefully out of his bed, wanting to take a rumpled sheet to wrap around her naked body but feeling that would make her look as if she was ashamed.

Which she probably was, but right now leaving was the best thing she could do, before he started asking questions.

Andy was far too astute for his own good!

But at the door she did turn to say thank you, adding honestly, as heat flooded her cheeks, 'I really needed that.'

He gave her a mocking smile that didn't quite hide the hurt she saw in his eyes.

'Any time. Only too happy to oblige.'

She fled, not wanting to make things more complicated than they already were. What they'd shared had been surprisingly intense and fulfilling for first time lovers, but that was all it could be. For all she knew, he had a woman in his life already.

And having a relationship with a colleague wasn't a good idea.

She showered, dressed for work, and came out to find him already gone. No doubt to the beach for his morning swim.

Images of his naked body danced before

her eyes and she knew she didn't want to be around when he returned, even though he'd not be entirely naked. She grabbed her things and headed for the café. Avocado and smoked salmon on toast sounded good, and if she kept her mind on food, and then on work, she wouldn't be thinking about how good it had felt to be held in Andy's arms— *or* what today's date meant to her and how hard she was going to find it…

CHAPTER FOUR

THEY WORKED THROUGH the day, carefully polite with each other but equally careful not to get too close. Fortunately, it was busy, some children transferred back to children's wards while new patients came in.

Two were high priority, one an oncology patient who'd received a stem-cell transplant from a non-family member and needed a total isolation room, which meant anyone entering the room, staff included, needed mask, gloves, booties and a long gown.

It was the mask Sam was having trouble with, in the small airlock area outside the isolation room. The strings had somehow become entangled with her hair and as someone else came in, she closed her lips tightly to capture the swear words that wanted to escape.

'Here, let me!'

His voice, right there behind her, stopped her breath, and the touch of his strong hands releasing her fingers and the tape from her hair stole her ability to breathe.

'It didn't mean anything, you know that, don't you?' The words tumbled out with a desperation she couldn't control. 'Can we forget it happened? I was upset, overwrought. The clock ticked past midnight and it just brought it all back. It's the anniversary, you see.'

He must have finished untangling her mask for now both hands rested on her shoulders, drew her back against his body.

'What happened?' he said gravely, and all the pent-up anxiety left her body in a long sigh.

'I can't talk about it today. But thank you, Andy,' she said quietly, then she stepped away because, contrary to what she had said, being held against him was extremely comforting.

Even enticing?

Definitely exciting to many parts of her body.

But she had to focus on work.

The small boy was Jake Andrews, and as Sam entered the room, he was sleeping. To one side sat the dedicated nurse, while on the other side his mother slept, not in a comfortable chair but on a narrow hospital bed, as sterile as the room itself.

While Andy examined their patient, Sam read through the notes, sighing again to herself when she realised what this child and his family had already been through. Superstitiously, she crossed her gloved fingers, hoping this time the treatment would succeed.

'I don't know that crossing gloved fingers works as well as un-gloved ones,' Andy murmured to her a little later as they stripped off their protective gear and threw it into the various bins.

She smiled and although her own body was asking what harm there'd be in a purely sexual relationship with him for a while, her brain was yelling to forget such folly. Andy hadn't the slightest interest in her. In fact, given how he'd felt about Nick's accident she was surprised that he seemed to tolerate her at all, let alone offer her a bed.

Although, as he'd said to her that first afternoon, she *was* the widow of his best friend…

And if that reminder filled her with a deep sadness, well, that was her problem.

She left the changing room, but Andy was close behind her.

'Our next arrival, Grant Williams, was riding his bicycle home from a mate's last night and was knocked over by a hit-and-run driver. It took a while to stabilise him, both at the scene and in the ED.'

'After which,' Sam guessed, 'he spent a good deal of time in Theatre getting put back together again.'

He'd also been put into an induced coma, Sam discovered when they reached his room, where his two anxious parents sat.

'Did someone speak to you about his condition?' she asked quietly, although both parents looked too shell-shocked to have taken much in.

'Broken pelvis, broken leg, fractured shoulder, cracked head,' the father recited, and was about to continue when Sam intervened.

'Did they tell you he's been put into an induced coma so he's deeply asleep, unconscious really, which will give his body, and particularly his brain, a little time to recover.'

'Someone said something,' the mother said quietly, and Sam smiled at her.

'What it means is that he won't regain consciousness until the specialists think he's well enough to cope with it all. That won't be for a few days, so although I know you want to be near him, you're better off going home and getting some rest. One of you might like to come back a little later just to sit and talk quietly to him, smooth his skin. But when the specialists decide to bring him out of the coma, we'll contact you so you can both be here, and you'll be the first people he sees.'

'What if we don't want to go home? If we both want to stay with our boy?'

The aggression in the man's voice suggested he was already exhausted so Sam knew she'd have to tread very carefully.

She was assembling her most persuasive arguments when she heard someone come into the room behind her and knew it was Andy.

'Of course you may stay if you wish,' he said, speaking directly to the father. 'But it's likely to be three or four days—perhaps longer—before the specialists decide to reverse the drug that's helping his body and mind deal with what happened. When that decision is made, we'll let you know so you can be here to reassure him he's safe.'

The father nodded and put his arm around his wife.

'Maybe the doctor's right, love,' he said. 'We'll be no good to him if we're exhausted, now, will we?'

She gave a wan smile but stood up at his urging, and after the lightest of kisses on her son's pale cheek left the room.

Sam was wondering why it still was—in a world where women often outnumbered men as doctors—that a man's explanation of a situation still held more weight. With other men, at least.

Musing on this, she missed the first bit of Andy's conversation.

'So I've a three-day conference in Sydney from tomorrow, but the welcome stuff starts this evening.'

She caught up as they followed the couple out the door. 'I wouldn't go if I felt you still needed me here, but you'll be fine.'

He walked away, paused, then turned to look at her, hesitating, before adding, 'I'll leave the car keys on the kitchen table—use it if you like.'

Another glance her way. 'And definitely use it if you're called out at night. I'll get a cab to the airport.'

Although, when she considered them again, those two looks towards her had told her everything, as well as his abrupt departure to a conference in Sydney.

He was ruling a line under what had happened between them the previous night, just as she had done earlier.

But would three days be enough for her body to get with the programme?

To stop fizzing with excitement at the sound of his voice and flaring with heat if he accidentally brushed up against her?

It had been bad enough discovering she was physically attracted to Andy when they'd met again, but it was far worse now, when every square inch of her skin knew the feel of his skin against it and seemed determined *not* to forget that night.

And yet…

Andy walked out through the front entrance to his apartment building, confident he'd find a cab cruising past. Confident, also, that he was doing the right thing—getting right away from the beguiling woman who was his best friend's widow,

He'd never been good with calendar dates so he hadn't had a clue that it had been the torturous pain of loss that had driven Sam into his arms the previous night. She'd been so willing, so hot really, responding with a ferocity he'd been foolish enough to believe was because she felt as much attraction to him as he did to her.

The intensity of the experience had stunned him, to the extent that his body felt as if she'd imprinted herself on his skin.

Cursing quietly under his breath, he threw his overnight bag into the taxi, pleased he had the diversion of a trip to Sydney, although Antarctica might have been a better option. But a couple of days away from the distraction that was Sam would help him get his life back on track—get things into perspective again…

Possibly!

He shook his head, so lost in his memories of the passion they'd shared he barely heard the cabbie's conversation.

Something about football, perhaps?

Left to her own devices, Sam visited the rest of her patients, discussing each of them with the dedicated nurse on duty with the child.

Whoever had trained these nurses in the fairly new hospital had done an excellent job because all the ones she saw today—and had seen earlier—were really invested in their patients, showing empathy as well as caring.

It was a special job, nursing in a PICU, and although the majority of nurses who chose to work there were empathetic, she'd known a few who just did their job—and did it well—but stayed detached from the child and his or her family.

And she was thinking about this, why? she wondered when she sat down at her desk to write up some notes and check the medication orders.

She knew the answer.

Thinking about anything was better than thinking about the previous night—and the way she'd behaved.

Like a wanton hussy, her old secondary school teacher would have said. Throwing yourself into that man's arms...

But that man was Andy, and although she'd seen less of him after her marriage she'd always been impressed by his dedication to his work—impressed by him as a genuinely nice person.

In fact, it had been his decision to leave the hurly-burly of the Emergency Department that Nick had loved so much to work in

Intensive Care and then Paediatric ICU that had influenced her own decision.

Though just why she was thinking of Andy on the anniversary of Nick's death, she wasn't sure. She pressed her hand against her flat stomach and forced her mind back to work.

A call from the nurse with the oncology patient killed any wayward thoughts and she went back to his room, gloved and gowned, and managed the mask herself this time before quietly opening the door.

Jake lay pale and wan on the bed, but a nasty rash was appearing on his torso.

'Have you called his oncologist? Sam asked, and the nurse nodded.

'It's most likely a reaction to one of the drugs he's on to suppress his immune system so his body doesn't reject the new stem cells, but I'll take some blood to test for infection.'

Sam was watching the monitor as she spoke, seeking any variation in the patterns of his heart rate or his blood oxygen level, listening to his chest, feeling the slightly raised nature of the rash.

She used a port in his left arm to extract some blood and labelled the three phials she'd taken while the nurse organised for someone to collect them from the changing room to get them to the laboratory as quickly as possible.

'Fluid overload,' Sam muttered to herself, and checked the drip to see how much fluid had gone into him since the last check, then his catheter bag to ensure he was getting rid of fluid.

Graft versus host disease was the most common complication and the rash could be a symptom of that. It was mostly seen within the first three months after a transplant but could occur up to three years afterwards.

She'd written up the information of all she'd done, including the tests she'd ordered, when the oncologist appeared and took the chart from her.

He was a silver-haired man with a tanned skin and a charming smile, and he spoke to young Jake like a family friend, reassuring the boy that they'd sort things out.

'What did you request with the bloods?' he asked Sam, turning away from the chart.

'Infection, low platelets, and any sign of organ failure,' she said, and he nodded.

'The results will be copied to me, and I'll be right back if they show anything. In the meantime, we might use a little more supplemental oxygen, and I'd suggest a simple mix of bicarbonate of soda and water on the rash to help ease the irritation.'

Sam smiled at him. 'It was my mother's panacea for all ills and certainly helped me survive chicken pox.'

The oncologist gave a theatrical shiver. 'Don't even think of things like that. The poor lad has enough possible complications without introducing childhood diseases. I'm thinking he might need another blood transfusion, but we'll wait for the test results. Then, of course, there's a possibility the stem cells didn't take, and he'll need more of them.'

Sam looked at the frail figure lying on the bed and prayed that the rash was nothing more than a reaction to one of the drugs coursing through his body in the drip fluid.

The nurse was already speaking to someone to arrange the soothing liquid and Sam would have left to see other patients, but she caught sight of Jake's mother gowning up in the anteroom, and waited to speak to her, to update her on what was going on.

For parents of children who were up to the stage of trialling bone-marrow transplants to save their child's life, the hospital processes were well known. They'd had to cope with the highs and lows of the previous treatments and procedures and the hope and despair that came with each one.

For Jake's mother, this was just one more bridge to cross, her faith in finding a cure for him never wavering.

Could she have handled that as well as most of the parents she saw did? Sam wondered.

If her child had lived…

She shut the memory down, but not before tears had pricked her eyes.

Three years today. It was stupid to even think about it!

But at least Andy hadn't been around to see her momentary weakness…

Andy boarded the plane for the short flight to Sydney with a strange sense of relief. Sam had drawn a line under what had happened the previous evening, which was, he was almost certainly sure, a good thing.

So why was he feeling a nagging sense of…

What?

Regret?

Not exactly…

No, he wouldn't think about it—particularly not how she'd felt in his arms, or the heat of her body as he'd slid into her—her cries of passion as she'd clung to him in that final release.

Get your head straight, Andy.

This was Sam! She'd needed comfort, and he'd been there to give it to her.

A tightening of his stomach muscles suggested that he was damned glad he *had* been there. Heaven forbid, she might have gone off with anyone!

Not, he told himself sternly, that it would have been any of his business if she had. He'd known she was grieving for Rosa, the child who'd died. That was only natural, all of them felt an unnecessary loss like that very deeply, but on top of the date of her own loss…

No, he couldn't begin to imagine what her feelings had been, and furthermore it was time to stop this pointless speculation and concentrate on the reason he was on the plane.

Not to escape Sam but to hear one of the US's top PICU physicians speak about making the experience for families more comfortable.

He prided himself on how well they did it at his hospital. He'd been consulted about it as it was being built, and, having spent so much time in hospital with his patient, smiling sister, he knew just how uncomfortable places they could be, and he'd had a raft of ideas to offer the designers. And you could always learn something from other hospitals, even if it was what not to do.

But his focus was obviously shot to pieces for surely one of the first among any '*not to do*' lists of his own was take your best friend's widow to bed!

Even if she'd been so willing, so excited, in turn both tender and torturous and loving, so totally irresistible he'd lost himself in her, lost all inhibitions, and had responded with a passion he knew he'd never experienced before.

He was jolted out of his heated memories as the plane landed in Sydney, and he shut the memories away.

He was here to learn, to pick up ideas to take back to his hospital that hopefully would produce better outcomes for his patients and their families.

His and Sam's patients—and *that* was definitely the last time he would think about her.

Today…

It was weird returning to Andy's apartment without him being there.

Weird and definitely unsettling!

There'd been a small, discreet 'Manager' sign on the door on the ground-floor apartment, opposite the café, and she'd thought it wouldn't hurt to ask about an apartment—maybe there'd be a one-bedroomed, which was all she'd need.

She knocked on the door, which was opened almost immediately by a youngish man with a slightly unkempt look about him who was clutching a puffy black garbage bag in one hand.

'Sorry, just on my way to the bins. I can't put this down without spilling the lot, so would you like to wait, or maybe walk with me?'

'I'm happy to do either, but all I really wanted to ask was whether you had an apartment for rent. Just for me.'

She found she'd fallen in beside him as she spoke, so kept walking.

'One bedroom?' he asked.

'Well, that's all I'd really need.'

She'd sleep on the couch if her mother came, but, given her mother's life, it wasn't all that probable.

'Yeah, there's one available,' he said, leading her down a concrete stairwell into the basement garage. 'But we're coming up to the Christmas holidays when all the empty apartments double in price. I'm only the manager for about forty different owners— most of them absentee owners—and some of them only rent out over Christmas, because that pays the bills on the place and they can use it themselves any time over the rest of the year.'

'So I'd be paying double normal price?'

'From next weekend when the season starts, yes,' he said, rather gloomily.

Intrigued, Sam asked, 'You don't like the holiday season?'

He shook his head. 'I don't dislike it,' he said, 'but it's just so much extra work, and the young people I employ for the season as cleaners also want to have fun so they're not exactly reliable.'

They'd reached the bins, corralled behind a high wooden fence, and he lifted the lid of one to dump the bag, before turning to a nearby tap to wash his hands.

'I do have a couple of rooms in my place I let out as B and Bs, only the second B is a chit for the café across the hall. They each have an en suite bathroom and a small open kitchen-cum-sitting area with a hotplate and a microwave and TV and such. If that'd suit you?'

'I think that would be more than enough for me,' Sam told him, and was about to shake his hand on the deal when she thought of Andy. Would he think her ungrateful?

Even rude?

'Can I let you know later?' she asked the manager as they emerged into the foyer once again.

'Sure, I'm Rod, by the way.'

Sam took his hand and shook it.

'Sam,' she said, and smiled at him.

'But you'd be living with a stranger—a man you don't even know,' Andy protested when she put the idea to him on his return on Saturday afternoon.

'I'm renting a room,' Sam corrected him. 'That's not exactly living with someone!'

'You could do that here,' he argued.

'Heaven knows, I don't need it, but you could pay rent if it would make you feel better.' He paused. 'It's because of what happened, isn't it?' he said, as grumpy as she'd ever heard the usually upbeat Andy.

'Not entirely,' she said. 'You know very well I've always intended to get my own place, and I like what I've seen of this area.' She hesitated. 'And, given you're the only person I know in this city, I thought it would be nice to be near you.'

'Just not in my apartment—in some other man's!'

Sam looked at him in disbelief. 'Andy, you're being ridiculous! The fact is, as Rod pointed out, summer holidays are a week away and rents on regular accommodation double for two months. He can't charge double for his rooms, so it works out well for me because it gives me a chance to settle in, get to know my way around, meet other people, make friends, then maybe, when the holidays end, find something permanent.'

She watched as he bit back the words she was sure he wanted to say, before muttering something about taking a shower and disappearing in the direction of his bedroom.

But did he *really* want her to stay?

Or was it simply a kindness to an old friend, something he was doing for Nick as much as her?

The question made her stomach hurt, as if, deep down, she'd wanted him to want her to stay for herself...

She shook her head, aware such thoughts were madness...

He *was* being ridiculous, and he knew it, but as Andy stalked off to his bedroom, it was all he could do to keep from grinding his teeth.

And his reason for this sudden, and quite irrational, anger?

He shook his head, not wanting to think about it, but still it gnawed away inside him, to the extent that he turned back towards the living room, where Sam stood at the window, silhouetted by the moon rising over the waters in front of her.

And, suddenly, he didn't want to argue with her—didn't want discord between them.

He walked closer, his footsteps on the timber floor causing her to half turn towards him.

'I thought it would be for the best,' she said, in such a small voice he knew he'd upset her with his tirade. 'I mean, it can't be helping your love life any, having me living with you. And maybe if I ever decide to chance such a thing again, it would be awkward for me as well.'

'What love life?' he snorted. 'That's not high on my list of priorities! Anyway, how many intensivists do you know who can manage a relationship successfully?'

'Plenty!' she snapped, any hurt she may have felt burned off by sudden anger. 'And this entire conversation is stupid. You took me in when I had nowhere to stay and for that I'm grateful, but it was never meant to be for ever and, providing I don't see any evidence of rats when I look at Rod's rooms tomorrow, I'm moving on. I've only delayed because I thought it would be polite to discuss it with you first. Not that this conversation has had any resemblance to a discussion.'

And this time it was Sam who stalked off, leaving him standing by the tall windows, gazing out to sea.

He'd heard—even understood—her final, angry words, but it was something she'd said earlier that had snagged in his mind.

Something about 'should she ever decide to *chance* such a thing again'…

'Chance' was a strange word for her to have used.

It implied risk. Had her marriage to Nick not been the nuptial bliss Nick had always made it out to be?

Had she found it harder than he had realised to live with Nick's mild OCD?

Though had it really been mild?

He shook his head.

Questions to which, he was reasonably sure, he'd never find answers, yet for some unfathomable reason he'd have liked to know...

CHAPTER FIVE

THE ROOM ROD offered Sam had a view out over the ocean and she was immediately entranced.

The bedroom was small, divided, she realised, in some clever way to make room for the small sitting room, a few cupboards, refrigerator, sink and microwave tucked into a corner, and to Sam's delight, a small barbecue out on the balcony, along with a couple of easy outdoor chairs and a table.

'It's perfect,' she told Rod, beaming with delight. 'I'll take it.'

'You're supposed to ask how much the rent is,' Rod reminded her, and Sam shook her head.

'I'm sure it's not over my budget. Not that I have a budget.'

But they did discuss the rent, and a good deal besides, out on the balcony, with the fresh north-easterly sea breeze cooling the air around them.

'So, you work with Andy,' Ron said, and Sam nodded.

'He's an old friend of my dead husband,' she explained. 'And he took me in when I arrived to save me going to a hotel while I got my bearings.'

'Nice,' Rod said. 'He's a good man.'

Something about the conversation was making Sam feel uncomfortable—talking about Andy with a stranger?—so she made the excuse that she'd need to pack her few things, took the keys Rod gave her and, after learning which key did what, she departed.

Andy, who'd been in a meeting when she'd left the hospital, was back when she walked in, new keys in her hand.

'Does your room have a lock?' he asked, looking at them dangling from her fingers.

She frowned at him, disturbed by the inference that she'd need a lock. To keep Rod out?

Surely not!

'You should change it,' Andy said, and Sam shook her head in disbelief.

'You think he'll come creeping into my room in the dead of night and ravish me?'

she snapped, the anger she'd thought she'd
learned to control sparking suddenly. 'I
should be so lucky!'

Really shouldn't have said that, she muttered in her head as she strode towards her
bedroom. It was just that Andy was being so
darned unreasonable about this. He should be
glad to be getting rid of her, not acting like
her moral guardian!

She shut the bedroom door and leaned
back against it, taking deep breaths to sweep
away the anger he'd aroused, especially as
the real reason she was moving out was because of him.

Well, not him as such, but the way she
was beginning to feel about him—and seeing him at home as well as at work—well, it
was just too much…

She had to pack.

She opened the door, intending to go out,
find Andy, apologise for losing her temper
then ask politely if she could borrow a suitcase for a few hours to stop her new clothes
getting crumpled and wrinkly in her old
backpack. But Andy was right there, outside the door, and her immediate reaction
was not suspicion about his presence but a
flood of attraction.

'I'm sorry!'

Their voices formed a chorus, but Andy recovered first.

'I don't know why I was upset,' he said. 'I guess I was kind of enjoying you being around. It's been a while since I've had company at home.'

Sam grinned at him.

'It's only been five days and you were away for two of them,' she pointed out, 'and, anyway, I'll still be around at work.'

He nodded but remained where he was—rooted in the passage.

Her turn to talk, obviously.

'I was wondering if I could borrow a suitcase just for this evening, to take my clothes down to Rod's.' She paused, before adding, 'And to say I'm sorry I lost my temper earlier.'

She tried a smile, but knew it was probably fairly pathetic. 'Every time I think I've conquered my wretched temper, something happens and I'm blowing up again.'

Another pause.

'Although you did provoke it, you must admit, talking about changing the locks!'

He laughed now, a joyous sound that made her toes curl inside her sneakers. She *so* had to get away from him, if only after work hours.

'So you're apologising but blaming me at the same time,' he teased, his eyes twinkling in such a way she had to forcibly clamp her hand to her side to stop herself reaching out and touching his face.

She *had* to move! Had to get away from this man who could have her hormones rioting with the twinkle in his eyes.

'I'll get you a case,' he was saying as he moved away from her, and she ran her hands through her unruly hair and clutched her head, trying to restore some balance to her mind in the hope it would do the same for her body.

He'd asked her to stay because she was Nick's widow and though he'd proved an exciting and satisfying lover when she'd thrown herself into his arms, that was no indication that he was in any way attracted to her.

In fact, the way he'd been so quick to agree with her about drawing a line under the incident proved that she was no more than an acquaintance—or friend at best...

And if that thought caused a tiny ache in her chest, then that was her problem, not his.

* * *

Andy dug into the back of his small store-room, dislodging a broom and mop he rarely used because he was blessed with a cleaning man who came once a week, and left his often untidy apartment spotless.

Was it because they'd had sex that he'd been behaving irrationally about Sam moving out?

Great sex, admittedly, but that's all it had been...

He'd answered a need in her, for which she was grateful, but she'd made it very clear that that was that. Which was just as well as he was having a lot of trouble working out just how he felt about Sam.

He was definitely attracted to her, now more than ever, it appeared. But attraction usually—well, often—led to love, and in his mind there was a huge blockage that would stop such a process.

Actually, there were two problems—the discomfort about her being his friend's widow, and the big one—what if she was still in love with Nick?

Would the latter explain her desperate need on the anniversary of his death?

She'd said she'd hated what she'd become

as his wife, but she'd also said she'd loved him to distraction.

And the way she'd said it suggested the love part had been paramount, so probably she still loved him.

Enough to stop her loving someone else?

Hell's teeth, get the suitcase and take it to her. Stop trying to fathom what's going on in someone else's head when you can't work out what's going on in your own. And given the mess you've made of the love business in the past, it certainly shouldn't be entering the equation.

You've given up on it, remember? Twice burnt by it. Surely that was enough for any man to realise he was better off single— free to enjoy brief encounters with willing women who might come his way.

He grabbed the suitcase and backed out of the small room, then pushed the case down the corridor, but his mind was right back on Sam, only this time he was telling himself he was done thinking about her—done guessing about her marriage and Nick and whether she still loved him.

Telling himself the easiest way to find out was to ask.

Right!

March up to Sam and say, 'Are you still in love with Nick?'

Honestly, man, for a supposedly intelligent human being you haven't got a clue!

He knocked on her door.

'I'll just leave the case here,' he said, but before he had time to turn away she'd flung open the door.

'Don't rush off,' she said, clearing a space on the bed between small piles of clothing. 'I won't be long, and I thought I could take you to dinner at the café as a thank you for having me.'

'You don't have to do that,' he said, but he did go into the room, sitting down where she'd made a space for him on the bed, watching her as she efficiently cleared the bed of clothing and packed it into the suit-case.

Watching her and wondering...

'I was only too happy to give you a bed.'

She looked up at him from where she knelt, a question in her eyes.

'Because I was your best friend's widow,' she said. A statement not a question after all.

'More than that, Sam,' he said. 'We'd been friends, you and I, back when we all met.' Even to him that sounded weak—mawkish—

so he quickly added, 'Besides which you were a new member of the team, and had nowhere booked to stay. I'd have offered the bed to whoever it was.'

'Okay,' she said, as if his explanation had sorted out something in her mind, which was good because it had only made him feel even more confused...

She turned her attention back to the packing, filling the edges around the neatly folded skirts and shirts with toiletries and, yes, the purple underwear!

He smiled to himself then realised she'd caught him for the rosy colour was rising in her cheeks.

'It's best I move,' she said quietly, then zipped the case shut and pulled it upright onto its rollers. 'But I'd still like to take you to dinner.'

He stood up and took the case, rolling it towards the door, turning to say, 'Ah, but I felt it was my turn to cook. I bought steaks and some stuff for a salad.'

'In a packet, no doubt?' she teased, and he felt a sense of relief—a sense that everything was all right between them again.

On the surface, at least.

Well, he'd just have to live with that.

Though in his heart he hoped that before too long they'd be able to talk—talk properly—about the past.

About their feelings?

And the future?

He shook his head. He and Sam may have enjoyed one glorious night of sex, but as far as she was concerned that was that. There'd been no suggestion—at any time really—that she might be feeling the same attraction towards him as he did towards her.

He'd grill the steak.

With her clothing installed in her new home, Sam returned to join Andy on his balcony, and now sat, sipping at a glass of white wine he'd produced, and watching him at the barbecue.

Out to her right, a low rising moon had silvered the ocean, whose soft murmur, this calm evening, filled her with a sense of peace.

A rare sense of peace, given she was with Andy.

But the muddle of emotions she usually felt with him—the attraction, the sense that it was wrong, the awareness that it probably wasn't reciprocated, especially now he *knew* she had been instrumental in his best friend's death—all those worries seemed to have slipped from her shoulders. Tonight she was just going to enjoy the sheer pleasure of being in a beautiful place with a friend.

'I feel good,' she said, and he turned to look at her, eyebrows raised.

Surprised?

'Well, you have to admit it's been a frenetic week,' she said. 'Getting here was bad enough, I kept worrying I wouldn't make it in time to start on Monday, then finding out you're my boss—which is good, don't get me wrong—then all the stuff with Rosa and the anniversary—my mind and body have been in turmoil.'

'And now?' he prompted, turning back to prod the meat—or just not wanting to look at her when she answered?

'Now I feel at peace,' she said. 'As if I can go forward into a whole new life stretching out in front of me. New hospital to work in, new staff to meet and get to know, and this beautiful town to explore. The beach, the sea, the sand—rock pools out on the headland, I'm sure—a whole new world.'

She paused, and as he carefully lifted the steaks onto two waiting plates, she added,

'I ran away, you see, after the accident. Couldn't face any of it, especially the thought of a life without Nick. But a couple of months ago, when I was offered a better post in London, I thought about it for, oh, all of two seconds, because I suddenly knew it was time to go home.'

'And now you're here?' he asked as he set the plates down on the table.

'I know it was the right decision, so really, why wouldn't I be feeling good?'

He nodded, as if satisfied with her answer and disappeared inside, reappearing with the salad bowl and cutlery and sitting down opposite her. 'Eat!' he said, smiling.

Which she did—they both did—so for a while there was no more talk and when it did resume it was work talk mixed with travel talk—his work in Boston, hers in London, comparisons of hospital systems, staffing arrangements. It was all nice, safe, work-related talk that skated fairly easily over the muddle of emotions she'd landed in when she'd met Andy again, and the mess she'd made of things the night Rosa had died.

They'd have to talk about that, too, sometime, she knew, but now to just sit in the soft moonlight with Andy, relaxed by the sound of the sea, was enough.

Might have to be enough always.

She pushed *that* thought away.

Jake's father was with him when they did their rounds on Monday morning, and looked as anxious as Andy felt. They didn't yet have the results of all the blood tests, but those they did have offered no clue as to what might have caused the rash.

Sam was explaining this to the father when Andy was paged to an emergency in the ED.

He excused himself and left Sam to get on with the round. She'd contact him if she needed any help. With the shift change on Thursday, they'd be working together less often, which, he decided as he made his way downstairs, would be a good thing. The urge to touch Sam, just lightly on the shoulder, as he'd left Jake's room had been almost overwhelming.

That, he reminded himself as he went down to the ED, was why relationships between colleagues could be difficult.

Even now, when he *wasn't* in a relationship with her, she was far too often in his thoughts and far, far too often those thoughts could be distracting.

And distraction was one thing a PICU physician just could not afford.

He was relieved when the elevator disgorged him outside the ED, and his focus returned immediately to work.

He heard, first, that it was a child saved from drowning, then, as he walked into the resus room, he realised the pale, anxious father was an old acquaintance—a fellow medical student he'd last seen in the Sydney hospital where Sam had been admitted after the accident.

Ned Radcliffe—the name came back to him as he held out his hand in greeting—but he could have been Santa Claus for all the notice Ned took of him. One hundred percent of his attention was focussed on the boy of about three who lay, unmoving, on the examination couch.

'Edward Radcliffe, two years four months, non-responsive when the ambos reached him,' a nurse said quietly to Andy. 'Father had been giving CPR, ambos took over and heart restarted. He's on oxygen, but he's remained deeply unconscious.'

'Any sign of a head injury?' Andy asked,

almost automatically, his mind on the child and how they might achieve the best possible outcomes for the small boy and his family.

'No, the ambos checked and the duty doctor here checked. Apparently, he went straight in.'

'How long would he have been in there, Ned?' Andy asked, and the father frowned as he heard the question, his eyes still on his son.

'I would say less than five minutes. I opened the pool fence gate to get a toy the dog had left in the garden, and turned to throw it back to the dog. But Chippy ignored it and raced back into the pool enclosure, barking like crazy, and that's when I realised Eddie must have followed me in.'

He looked at Andy now and frowned, then said, 'Andy?' in a bewildered voice.

'That's right, Ned. I'm head of the PICU here. We'll be admitting Eddie. He'll get the best of care.'

He turned back to the child, considerably pleased by the knowledge of such a short immersion.

'Hello, Eddie,' he said, in a loud voice, but there was no response, not even when he clapped his hands beside the little head.

Neither did Eddie retract his foot when Andy stuck a pin into the sole of it, testing for physical response.

'We'll take him to Radiography on the way up to the PICU. I'll order an EEG and MRI,' he said to the nurse as he wrote up the requests. 'Do you want to stay with him, Ned?'

Ned nodded. 'I'll phone my wife on the way, let her know what's going on.'

He looked at Andy, a plea for reassurance in his eyes. 'Do you think…?'

Andy patted him on the shoulder.

'You were right there on the spot and did the best possible thing in giving CPR immediately. His heartbeat returned quickly, and he wasn't in the pool for long. They're all good indicators, Ned.'

An orderly arrived to transfer the boy, via Radiography, to the PICU, so Andy returned to the ward, aware the radiography he'd ordered probably wouldn't show much at this stage but still wanting a baseline from which to work.

He found Sam at the desk, and told her what was happening, asking if she'd known Ned.

She shook her head, but obviously hadn't taken much notice of the question because she asked, 'Would you consider continuous EEG monitoring?'

He shrugged. 'I'd been thinking of it, why?'

She grinned at him. 'I often wonder if it does much good and I think it must freak most parents out, seeing all those electrodes attached to their child's head. It's almost yelling "brain injury" at them.'

He shook his head. 'I must admit I've never thought of that aspect to it, but I'm really hoping he'll be responsive by the time he gets up to us.'

'And his father—this Ned—was he at university with you?' Sam asked, aware she'd usually have put an 'and Nick' at the end of that question.

But the peaceful, pleasant evening she'd enjoyed with Andy the previous night had left her more aware of Andy than when she'd been living with him.

And *that* had been bad enough!

Then she'd been able to put it down to proximity, especially after the night together, but now she was beginning to wonder if the awareness was more than physical attraction—not that she was even going to think about the L word.

Love had been too hard, like a prison she couldn't escape.

The arrival of young Eddie blocked all extraneous thoughts from her mind, especially as his father was beaming with joy.

'He reacted to the noise of the MRI in spite of the earmuffs,' he told them, although the little boy lay still, eyes closed again.

'He opened his eyes and moved his legs.'

'That's great, Ned, but we'll still keep him here and do further tests. The bloods should be back soon, and they'll tell us more, but everything is looking positive for the moment.'

'I'll phone my wife,' Ned said, and disappeared out of the room.

'He didn't want us to see him crying,' Sam said softly.

'And you,' Andy asked, looking intently into her eyes. 'Are you worrying again about the myriad things that can endanger a child and how a parent can protect them from everything?'

She shot him a quick smile. 'No, I was thinking how lucky they were to have such an intelligent dog!'

And with that she walked away, because

of course she'd been worrying about how parents managed to survive their children's childhoods, Though the likelihood of her ever having to go through such agony was diminishing fast.

She'd known when she'd chosen to go into intensive care that it would be six hard years before she became qualified, then another six months before she qualified for paediatric intensive care. She'd done those final six months in London and had stayed another six months because the hospital had offered so many learning opportunities.

So now, at thirty-five, it wasn't that she was running out of time to have a child, but running out of time to have children—a family, something she'd dreamed about since she'd been a child herself, brought up by a single mother who'd been banished from her own family as a disgrace.

CHAPTER SIX

SAM WAS STANDING at the monitor desk, checking through some lab results, when she saw Ned again, returning to the hospital, this time with a woman she guessed must be his wife.

He stopped to introduce her to Sam, who was slightly startled when the woman said, 'Oh, I know who you are.'

'Oh, yes?' Sam said politely.

'Yes, of course. You were the new doctor at the hospital where Nick and Andy worked and they both fancied you. You must remember, Ned—they tossed a coin to see which one would ask her out and Nick won. How is Nick, by the way?'

'Nick was killed in an accident three years ago,' Sam said, but her mind was whirling.

He and Andy had actually *tossed up* to see who asked her out?

For some reason, the idea disturbed her. Made her feel like a cheap prize at a funfair.

The woman, whose name she'd forgotten almost as soon as she'd heard it—was it Ann?—and Ned were now arguing about whether or not he'd been in the pub that night, making Sam feel even worse.

Although, she decided, maybe it was keeping their minds off their concerns for Eddie.

'Eddie's doing well,' she said, glad to have found a way to interrupt things she didn't want to hear. 'You must both be pleased.'

But it didn't help much as Ann was now berating her husband for his carelessness in letting little Eddie fall in the pool.

'We *are* pleased,' Ned said, ignoring his wife's accusations with an ease that suggested they argued often. 'How long do you want to keep him in?'

'Overnight at least,' Sam told him, then watched as he steered his wife, still talking, to Eddie's room.

She moved on to see Jake, who was brighter today, his test results showing positive signs that the stem-cell transplant had taken. His father was with him today, explaining to Sam that he'd taken some personal time off work so his wife could have a proper rest at home.

'With two other children, it's hectic, but both our sets of parents help out all they can. My mum's staying with us at the moment, and the other kids love it as she spoils them rotten, doesn't she, Jake?'

Jake smiled, and touched his father's gloved hand.

'Me too,' Jake said, and pointed to a stuffed alligator that looked ready to eat the child.

Andy came into the changing cubicle as she was pulling off her gown, and although her body felt the usual rush of attraction that was becoming part of her normal life, it was Ann's earlier words that came back to her.

'Did you and Nick actually toss a coin to decide which of you would ask me out?' she demanded as pique at such behaviour overcame the silly attraction thing.

'Not at all,' Andy said, in an offended tone. 'We did rock, paper, scissors!'

Sam frowned at him, aware he thought the whole thing a joke, but feeling…slighted by it?

'And after you lost, that was it?' she muttered at him, as she hauled off the rest of her protective gear. 'You must have been really keen!'

And without waiting for a reply, she stalked out of the tiny room.

But once away from Andy, she tried to understand why hearing the silly nonsense had upset her so much.

It had been years ago, she'd married Nick, so how or why he'd asked her out shouldn't matter a jot.

A call from the ED made her push the past away, although she was aware it would niggle away deep inside her no matter how much she ignored it.

'We've isolated another girl, and the red spots in her mouth with their tiny pinpricks of white in the centre confirm it's measles,' Phil, the young intern on duty, told her as she came into the emergency department.

He led the way to one of the two isolation rooms in the ED and introduced the patient, Ruby, and her parents, Alice and Bob.

Not knowing the local area, Sam asked the intern to stay so they could try to work out if the two cases were connected in any way.

While she examined the little girl, a year older than Rosa had been, she listened to Phil's questions, and from the way he shook his head she realised there wasn't an obvious overlap in the two children's activities or friends.

'I'll admit her to our Paediatric Intensive Care unit,' Sam told the parents, 'but that's just because we can isolate her better than on the normal children's ward, where the contagion could spread.'

She left instructions on the chart and returned to the PICU, her mind puzzling over this second admission. She knew immunisation rates in the country as a whole were above ninety percent—she'd looked it up when Rosa had been admitted—yet two children in a regional city, two children out of the—at the most—ten percent not immunised had contracted the disease.

'Who does what?' she asked Andy, when she caught him in the staffroom and explained her concern. 'Do the Infectious Diseases people have staff who follow the trail of the two children, or do the police do it, or do we do it?'

Andy frowned at the question, and as she looked at him the question of whether she'd have gone out with him if he'd won their stupid game popped into her head.

Forget it!

But she knew she probably wouldn't have. Knew it was the kind of question that could bob into her head as she fell asleep at night or walked on the beach, thinking of nothing in particular.

'I think the infectious diseases staff use the police if they need them,' Andy was saying, while her mind wandered. 'We'll inform them of this second case, and they can publicise it, warning parents of the dangers, suggesting unimmunised children should be done before it becomes more widespread.'

'Has there been anything special here recently?' Sam asked. 'A local agricultural show, surfing contest people might have watched, a circus, or funfair of some kind?'

'Somewhere people from all walks of life could have met,' Andy said, more or less to himself. 'You're right, that's something they'll look into, I'm sure. And there *was* the annual show about a week before you came, and it had a big sideshow alley and all the fun of the fair.'

'I think I'd rather you said there'd been nothing like that, because if it came from a travelling fair anyone could be the carrier, and who knows where they went next.'

He grinned at her, which made her think

she *would* have gone out with him—way back when...

'Which makes me doubly glad it's someone else's job to locate him or her,' he was saying. 'Have you admitted the new case?'

'She should be on her way up. Her name's Ruby, and she's not as feverish as Rosa was, but I thought it best to keep her away from other children so she'll go into another of our isolation rooms.'

'I'll see her before I go,' Andy said, and Sam realised with a slight shock that this was the first day of a new shift. She'd known about it, had it noted in her diary, knew exactly when she would and wouldn't be at work, but suddenly Andy was departing and, for all she'd have a registrar or a young resident on duty with her at all times, she'd be in charge.

Andy must have read what she was thinking in her face, for he reached out and touched her shoulder.

'You handled it all extremely well when I was in Sydney, remember, and I'll only be a phone call away,' he told her. 'It's the paperwork more than the patients that'll get you down!'

'I'll be fine,' she said, as forcefully as

she could, but again guessed he'd read her doubts.

'Of course, you will,' he assured her. 'And you're off on Sunday—well, on call—so bring your phone and I'll take you for a drive around the place if you like, show you some of the sights of the great Port Fortesque!'

'That sounds good,' Sam said, although she had more doubts about that plan than she did about running the department in his absence.

Andy walked away, not at all concerned over Sam's ability to keep the place running, more concerned that she'd been upset over his and Nick's silly bet.

But she *had* agreed to go out with him on Sunday, although as he was the only person she knew in the area, that didn't mean much.

He went back to his office and tidied his desk, then decided to call in on young Eddie before he left.

His mother was sitting with him, reading a story to the bright, alert child.

'He could really come home now, couldn't he?' she said, smiling sweetly at Andy.

'Tomorrow,' he said firmly. 'We want some follow-up bloods and another EEG, but Dr Reilly will discharge him tomorrow, probably by eleven-thirty.'

'Oh, pooh!' the woman said. 'I was hoping Sam would be off duty tomorrow. I was going to ask the two of you to dinner at the weekend. Ned was so pleased to meet up with you again, especially as we're new in town. He's just joined a practice on the north side. I didn't want to leave Sydney, but he thought it would be better to bring Eddie up in the country.'

She gave a theatrical shudder and added, 'This was a compromise, and look what just happened.'

Andy closed his eyes and thanked the merciful fates that Sam was not around because he was pretty sure she wouldn't want this gossipy woman—it had to be she who'd told Sam about the rock, paper, scissors fiasco—linking their names like that.

He checked Eddie's file, spoke briefly to the bright little boy, and escaped before Ann could think of another plan.

'Would you have asked me out if you'd won the bet?'

It was the first question Sam asked when she climbed into his car on Sunday morning, dressed in pristine white slacks and a black and white striped shirt, her usually unruly hair somehow knotted rather severely on the top of her head.

Her question had come just in time to stop him saying she looked terrific and Andy had to concentrate on getting out of the underground garage far more intently than he needed to. But once on the road, taking the one that led to the lighthouse first, he knew he'd have to answer.

'Of course,' he said.

He didn't need to glance her way to know she was frowning—he could actually feel her tension in the air.

'But couldn't you have asked at another time?'

The question made him frown.

'Once you were going out with Nick? Of course not!'

'Because I was somehow marked as his?' she demanded, as he pulled into the parking area near the track that led to the top of the headland.

He turned to face her, puzzled by the question—trying to think back to that fateful time.

'Not marked as his—I don't think I

thought that way. It's just, well, you were going out with him—why would I assume you'd say yes to me? And how would he have felt if I'd done such a thing? And what would he have thought of you—well, of us both— if you'd said yes? Life just doesn't work that way.'

She'd been staring out the window at the sea, but as she turned back towards him he wanted to ask her if she would have said yes, but it was all so pointless.

'What happened, happened,' he said, reaching out to touch her cheek with one finger. 'There aren't any set rules or guidelines for life, you know. We just have to stumble along as best we can, doing what we feel is right at the time, and hopefully not having too many regrets when we look back at the past.'

She smiled and touched her hand to his.

'We tend to remember the regrets—the bad things, more than the good, don't we?' she said, giving his hand a squeeze before opening the car door, signalling, without a doubt, that that particular conversation was over.

They climbed the hill to the top of the rocky outcrop, coming out on the grassy knoll with the wide Pacific Ocean stretching out on both sides of them.

Sam threw her arms wide and turned to him in sheer delight.

'This is what I dreamt about—all the time I was in London, and while I was with Mum in the wilds of South-East Asia. I dreamt of living near the ocean. Working in Perth gave me a taste for it, for being close to the sea and beaches—although with my skin I really should have stayed in London or gone even further north to Scotland. But I think Aussies need the ocean—well, I do,' she said, her face aglow with the wonder of it.

So it seemed natural to take advantage of those out-flung arms and wrap his around her body, holding her close—a friendly hug—for all his body screamed for more.

They drew apart but somehow were holding hands, and walked across the grass to the brilliant white lighthouse and the squat building that had been the keeper's cottage nestled beside it.

They climbed to the top and from there looked back over the countryside that surrounded the sprawling coastal city.

'It's mainly dairy farms, some cattle properties and plenty of hobby farms, where people keep everything from goats to llamas,' he told her. 'There are local markets on the second and fourth Sunday of the month. You'd be surprised what you can buy there. Everything from local wines and beers, to hats, and mats, and guinea pigs.'

'Well, that's next Sunday accounted for,' she said. 'And next Saturday or maybe on one of my early finish days next week, I want to have a look for a car, just something small to get me to the hospital at night when I'm on call.'

She turned to him and put her finger against his lips.

'Don't bother telling me I can always take yours,' she said, 'because I wouldn't dream of it. And, anyway, you might be using it.'

She frowned, as if about to say more, but other people arrived at the top and the moment passed.

Could this count as courting? he wondered as they made their way back to the car, her hand still captive in his.

Such an old-fashioned word, but he couldn't remember ever being so uncertain with a woman—uncertain how to proceed, wondering whether, if he rushed things, he might spoil what they already had—which *had* to be friendship.

But if he were to court her, start with occasional dates maybe…

Dear God, it all seemed so infantile when they were both mature people and had already slept together!

But he couldn't help but be aware of the distance she usually kept between them; her avoidance of an accidental touch, let alone a real one. And instinct told him it was to do with her marriage, her previous experience that had either been so great she'd never stopped loving Nick, or so tricky she didn't want to repeat it.

Could he ask?

Get her to talk about it?

Not really, when either love or loyalty to Nick would colour her reply. And given the failure of love in *his* life, he doubted he'd be able to judge which it was.

And, to be honest, he'd been wary of proximity himself—of getting too close, of touching her by accident.

Yet, still hand in hand, they reached the car, and the mood was broken.

'Nick would have asked me out if you'd won,' Sam said quietly, and Andy felt his gut clench as the words told him with a stark certainty that Nick was never far from her thoughts.

Sam used the excuse of needing to shop for food and sort out her new living quarters to turn down Andy's invitation to spend the afternoon at the local gallery before an early dinner—even just fish and chips by the shore.

The morning had been confusing enough.

Spending non-work time with Andy had been wonderful and having seen more of this beautiful place where she'd ended up had made her delighted with her decision.

But Andy's hug, the hand-holding had stirred up memories of their night together, and her body ached for more intimacy—for kisses and touches, for being held, and whispered words…

But to get more involved with Andy was really impossible. In Andy's mind this might appear to be a prelude to marriage and even after three years the M word brought up an image of a black hole into which she'd disappear.

Andy was as different from Nick as it was possible for a man to be, and he'd be a loving, supportive husband and wonderful father to the children she really wanted to have.

But would *she* change, as she had with Nick?

She didn't blame Nick for the person she'd become within the marriage because it had been something she hadn't liked in herself. She'd felt as if she was always trying to prove something, and somehow always failing...

Growing up with only a mother and with no extended family around by which to judge people's marriages, she'd had no idea she'd find it as overwhelming as she had.

But Andy was different, and having found her way back to being herself again, surely she wouldn't lose that with Andy.

Would it be a risk?

She'd been lying on her bed while these thoughts had worked their way through her head, coming back now to the fact that it would be wrong to have an affair with Andy because he'd be hurt when she ended it. And, what's more, she'd have to find another job, as working with him afterwards would be just too hard.

Actually, working with him during an affair would also be hard—the discretion part of it almost impossible, and that, too, would damage Andy more than her.

And wasn't all this futile? Hand-holding hardly counted as a declaration of love!

She climbed resolutely off the bed, changed into one of her new swimming costumes, slathered fifty-plus sun block all over her skin, pulled on a light shift as a cover-up, and headed for the beach.

An hour battling the waves would chase all these gloomy thoughts away. And, besides, Andy might just have been holding her hand because they were friends.

She slipped on her sandals, slapped on her hat and, with a towel slung over her shoulder, she set off.

Perhaps if she talked to Andy about these things it would help.

Or would she be making a complete fool of herself, if he wasn't the slightest bit interested in her—even attracted to her?

Just because he had been once, it didn't mean much six years later...

Hoping an hour out on the waves would clear his head and tangled thoughts, Andy changed into board shorts and a light wetsuit, went back to the garage to get his board from the lock-up section in front of his car, and headed for the beach.

He was sitting on his board out beyond the breakers, hoping for one last good wave to carry him all the way back to the beach. If it didn't come, he'd paddle into shore, but it was so peaceful and serene out here, he didn't mind a wait.

The wave, when it did come, was a beauty, and he caught the top of it before it curved into a barrel, crouching on the board to get his body into this green curl of the ocean, exultant as he rode out the other end.

A loud cheer from the beach told him he wasn't alone, and as he rode the wash of the now-broken wave through to the sand, he realised it was Sam.

'I didn't know you could surf,' she said, then frowned. 'In fact,' she added in a puzzled voice, 'I really know nothing about you—the now you, not the six-years-ago you. I've been rude, babbling on about me and my travels, but what of you?'

She'd stretched her towel on the beach and was sitting on it, spreading sunscreen on her arms and legs—long, long, and quite lovely, legs.

'Who are you, Andy Wilkie?' she said,

smiling up at him as he stripped off the top half of his wetsuit, letting it dangle from his waist, and picked up his towel. 'And what have *you* been doing? I know we talked briefly about Boston and our travels. In fact, I read a paper you wrote from there—the dangers of hyperthermia in children, I seem to remember. But the real Andy Wilkie. You're not married, unless you have a wife tucked away in a cupboard somewhere, so what's been happening in your life?'

She patted the sand beside her, and when he'd dried off his face and torso he sat down next to her. She'd obviously been swimming, for her hair hung in wet tendrils down her back, and clustered ringlets curled around her face.

'Did you ever marry?' she asked, bringing his attention back to what was obviously going to be an inquisition.

'Got close to it twice,' he said, and immediately felt guilty that he'd said it so casually—with such a lack of feeling.

But wasn't it the truth?

'Wrong women?' Sam persisted, and this time, looking at her as he answered, he could say truthfully, 'Maybe I was the wrong man.'

'I doubt that,' she said. 'You're one of the

good guys, but I assume that took up quite a bit of the six years, wooing and winning not one but two wrong women. But there has to be more—a grand passion?'

That he definitely wasn't going to answer!

'Several not so grand passions,' he did say, because he didn't want her persisting. 'But fun relationships with no expectations at the end of them. Really, Sam, you must know yourself how hard it is to keep a relationship alive when one, or in my case often both, the parties are involved in either emergency medicine or PICU.'

'We should have been skin specialists— they hardly ever get called out at night,' she said, but she was smiling, and he knew her passion for the job they did was as strong as his.

It was time to change the conversation, but he'd missed his chance. Sam was already asking, 'Were there reasons?'

He looked blankly at her. 'Reasons for what?'

She gave an exasperated sigh. 'For neither of the relationships going on to marriage? And don't talk to me about work pressures. The majority of specialists in all fields man-age to make marriage work and the ones who don't probably wouldn't have stayed married if they were bank managers or garbage collectors.'

'Garbage collectors?' he echoed, and she had to smile.

'You know perfectly well what I mean! What happened?'

Tell her, or not tell her?

He thought how peaceful this was—or had been—just being with Sam, enjoying her company and the beautiful setting. Medical matters had been the last things on their minds.

So he told another truth...

'I just wasn't right for them,' he said, 'or perhaps they weren't right for me. It was a long time ago, Sam, and I've settled into a life I'm comfortable with—comfortable in. I like my life just as it is. Work does have pressures, as you know, and to be able to come home and just relax and renew myself is exactly what I need.'

Liar, a voice was yelling in his head, although it was only a partial lie. He really *did* like his nice, uncomplicated lifestyle.

'Nonsense,' Sam told him. 'You've got to get out and about. You're far too good a man to be frittering your life away on brief romances. You'd make a wonderful father—anyone who sees you with a patient would realise that in an instant!'

He could tell she was winding up towards more marital advice, so it really *was* time to change the conversation.

'So now you've obviously done all you needed to do in your enormous new living space,' he said to her, 'you've got no excuse—so how about fish and chips on the beach? I know the best fish and chip shop in Port F.'

And to his surprise she smiled, and said, 'You're on! But I like calamari and chips if that's okay, and I do need to shower and do something to control my hair before we can leave. Will we walk?'

'It's not too far,' he said, his mind racing ahead to the possibility of holding hands—if not on the way there, at least on the way back.

You are nuts, he told himself, but his mind had already moved on to a dark spot at the end of the esplanade that would be perfect for a very chaste kiss...

But right now she was standing up so he picked up her towel, took it a little further downwind on the beach and shook the sand from it before handing it back to her.

She seemed surprised by the gesture but simply thanked him, then wrapped the towel around her body, covering her swimsuit but leaving the lovely length of leg for him to enjoy.

Which he probably shouldn't be enjoying as much as he was.

'Are you checking out my legs?'

Sam's sudden question brought him out of this consideration.

'Yes, I was,' he told her, 'and very lovely legs they are too. And you must remember it's allowable on Aussie beaches for men to admire women's legs. It's one of the reasons we have beaches!'

She laughed and told him he was talking nonsense, but the colour in her cheeks suggested she hadn't minded it, nonsense or not!

They *did* hold hands, and although Sam suspected Andy had used the excuse of helping her up the first steep hill to take hers, she found it was comfortable, her fingers wrapped securely in his, and did nothing to stop the small pleasure.

They ate their paper-wrapped meals sitting on a bench that overlooked the river, dog walkers strolling by, seagulls clamouring around their feet for the occasional dropped scrap.

And they talked of work—Sam bringing Andy up to date on the progress of their current patients, explaining that Ryan had picked up quite a lot and could possibly go home the following day.

'Although you know him better than I do. So I decided to leave that decision to you.'

She fed her last chip to the clamouring seagulls and crumpled up the paper.

'Have you enjoyed it?' Andy asked, and she smiled at him.

'The fish and chips by the river? Enormously!' she said.

He grinned at her, sending tendrils of delight threading through her body.

'You know very well we were talking about work!' he scolded. 'Have you enjoyed your first two weeks?'

She turned to him.

'Loved it,' she said. 'And that's mainly thanks to you for making it so easy for me to fit in.'

He looked at her for a moment, then said, 'I think you'd fit in anywhere.'

They walked back, Andy leading her to a track that would take them up through the scrub to the top of the hill near the apartment block. But when he stopped beneath a dramatic pandanus palm, and drew her into his arms, she looked into his dimly lit eyes and had to ask, 'Are you courting me?'

His answer was a light kiss on her lips.

'Would you like me to?'

She shook her head, unable to really answer that, but she nestled closer to his body, finally pulling away enough to say, 'I'm not sure I'm good courting material, Andy.'

'Because?' he asked, kissing her cheek, then the hollow beneath her ear.

'I wasn't good at marriage,' she blurted out, because Andy's kisses were tantalising, and her body, as well as her brain, was going haywire. 'I loved Nick, but it wasn't enough somehow. And I lost myself somewhere in it. Mum was away, in South America most of the time, but I doubt she'd have been much help, because she'd never been in a long-term relationship. And how could I ask a friend how their marriage worked?'

He kissed her lips again, and before she dissolved into the bliss of being kissed by

Andy—which she had done all too recently—
she eased away again.

'Nick wouldn't have been easy to live
with,' Andy pointed out, still holding her
loosely in his arms.

'That's no excuse for my failure,' Sam told
him, her voice thick with remembered un-
happiness. 'I just don't know, Andy.'

He turned, but kept one arm around her
waist as he steered them both back onto the
path.

'I doubt you lost of all of yourself,' he said
gently, 'because to me you're every bit the
Sam I used to know, only wiser, but just as
fierce in protection of something you believe
is right, and passionate about your patients.'

'Doesn't mean I'm good marriage material, though,' she said gloomily.

'Well,' he said, 'as I've already told you, I
didn't even make it to a wedding, so I can't
judge anyone else. But do we have to look
that far ahead? What about now?'

Sam was tempted, so tempted, yet still
something held her back.

'We're colleagues,' she reminded him.

'And surely professional enough to keep
our work lives separate?' he countered. 'So

forget about the future and let's try just for now?'

She wished she could see his face, but the track was narrow and dark so he led her by the hand, about half a step ahead.

Just for now. The words echoed in her head, sounding far too tempting, while somewhere deep inside her body some traitorous little impulse was dancing up and down with joy at the thought of an affair with Andy.

But whether either of them could do 'just for now' without someone getting hurt was a totally different question.

They came out on the top of the hill, meeting up with the reality of streetlights, apartment blocks and occasional traffic.

'You don't have to decide this right now,' Andy told her, wrapping his arm around her waist again now they could walk side by side. 'Just think about it for—oh, a few minutes, maybe an hour?'

He was smiling, sure they'd reached the place he wanted to be, but still caution held her back.

'Tomorrow,' she said, 'and, because I'm not nearly as sure as you are about the "professional at work" side of things, I'll tell you when you knock off tomorrow.'

'What about when your shift ends, then?' he said with a smile, and she shook her head.

'I'm on early, as you well know, and I'm going out to look at cars when I finish work, so we'll leave it till your shift ends, thank you very much. I'll even cook us dinner if I can use your kitchen, and perhaps your balcony to eat on.'

She could see his face now, and guessed he was holding back an urge to say he'd look at cars with her, or maybe they wouldn't need two cars, but he did hold back, and she squeezed his hand.

Maybe it *would* work out—if only just for now…

CHAPTER SEVEN

SAM LOVED EARLY-MORNING SHIFTS. The wards were quiet, lacking the buzz and bustle that seemed to build up during the day, and many of the children were still asleep.

Those who were awake were usually chatty. Kayla, her diabetes now stabilised with the knowledge and drugs she'd need to keep it that way, was due to go to the wards, where she'd spend a day with one of her parents and a specialised nurse to run through the pin-prick blood test she'd need to do several times a day with her special device, and practise using the syringe with which she'd be injecting her insulin.

Sam sat with her for a few minutes, talking to her about what lay ahead, reassuring her that she'd soon be able to manage it all without stress, telling stories of six-year-olds she'd seen who had been doing their own injections for a year.

Then on to Grant, who was due to be brought out of his coma today. So much rested on this, although evidence of mild brain damage might not be noticeable for some time.

But the shock for the child, waking to find so much plaster on his body, one leg suspended above the bed by a sling around his ankle, his other leg held together with an external frame, would be the most immediate problem.

'How do I explain it all to him?' his mother, who was sitting by the bed, asked.

Sam smiled at her. 'With any luck he'll find it exciting—something to tell all the kids at school. But he'll be woozy for a day or two, so don't get alarmed. As far as all our tests show, there was no substantial damage to his brain, just some slight swelling, which has gone down now.'

She waved her hand towards the sling.

'Boredom's going to be the main thing—he's not going to be able to move around much for a while. Does he have some kind of device with games on that he can use while lying in bed?'

His mother gave a huff of rueful laughter.

'He has some hand-held thing he plays with all the time. In fact, I feel so guilty because that's why he was out on his bike. I told him if he didn't put the silly device away and get out in the fresh air, I'd confiscate it for good.'

'You can't blame yourself,' Sam told her, knowing it would do no good at all. How often had she told herself she wasn't to blame for Nick's death when she knew full well it was the argument that had caused it.

It wasn't rational, she knew that, but it lingered anyway, as this would with Grant's mother...

Abby was sufficiently recovered to be transferred to a ward, and Sam was writing up the protocols for it when a shiver down her spine told Andy had just walked into the room.

'You're early,' she said, not turning to look at him in case her too-ready blush gave her away.

'Wanted to see Abby before she left us,' he said, going to stand by the bed and taking Abby's hand.

'Happy to be getting out of here, Abs?' he said, and the girl smiled radiantly at him.

'But I'll miss you all,' she said, the words belying the smile. 'You've all been so kind, especially you, Dr Wilkie!'

Now *she* was blushing, and Sam bumped Andy's arm as they left the room.

'Do all the teenage girls fall for you, Dr Wilkie?'

'Behave yourself,' Andy said sternly, but the twinkle in his eyes told her how hard this 'just colleagues thing' could prove to be.

'Why *are* you here early?' Sam asked, as they stood outside the door, the file in Sam's hands between them so it *could* look like a normal colleague conversation.

'Paperwork,' he said briefly, but she knew it was more than that.

He'd wanted to see her just as much as she'd wanted to see him, and how they were both going to get through their shifts when the air between them was so charged it was a wonder the lights weren't flickering.

'Go do your paperwork!' Sam said, needing to get away from him so she could sort out what was going on in her head *and* her body.

He left, but it didn't help much.

How hadn't she felt this charge last night, when they'd been so serious and adult about not committing too much? How stupid had that been? Surely if they'd gone to bed last night, she'd have been satisfied enough not to want to rip his clothes off in the hospital corridor this morning.

Focus!

She forced Andy from her mind and concentrated on the patients, possibly a little too hard because one mother asked her if everything was all right in the panicky voice parents got when a doctor was looking worried.

'She's fine,' Sam said. 'I was just wondering if she was ready to go to a children's ward today or to leave it until tomorrow.'

'It would suit me better tomorrow,' the mother told her, 'so I can bring in some everyday clothes for her. I noticed when someone showed me the ward she'll be going to that the children were in day clothes, not pyjamas.'

'Then tomorrow it is,' Sam said. 'And you're right, she'll feel more at ease if she's wearing day clothes like the others.'

It was a nothing conversation, but it brought Sam's mind back into balance. This was work, and her mind was now firmly fixed on it, and would remain there for the rest of the shift.

Which, as it turned out, was a nightmare.

A call from the ED with a third measles case, this time a boy of eleven. Sam went straight down and although the boy wasn't particularly sick, she knew he could deteriorate. Plus the fact that they could isolate him best in the PICU meant she had a new patient.

Peter Collins—a nice-looking kid—was obviously unhappy about being in hospital.

'But I'm not that sick!' he complained to Sam, when she visited him on his arrival in the PICU.

'We don't want you spreading the disease any further,' Sam told him, as she read through the information the ED had collected on him.

'It says here he has had all his immunisations,' she said, turning to Mrs Collins who was telling Peter to behave himself. 'Did they include measles?'

Mrs Collins nodded. 'I'm sure they did—we had to show the papers to his kindy—but I don't know what happened to them after that. It was years ago.'

'Well, it might explain why he's not as badly affected as the other two,' Sam said. 'But we're trying to track the source. Did

Peter go to the show that was on here not long ago?'

Mrs Collins nodded. 'We all went. It was just after Peter's birthday and some of the family had given him money to go on all the rides.'

'Can you remember what rides you went on?' Sam asked her patient, then had to listen to how rad the dodgem cars were and why he hadn't gone on the Ferris Wheel—far too high and he'd have been sick—but had loved the ghost train, and the hall of mirrors, but mostly he'd been on the dodgems.

Sam shook her head.

The other two children were surely too young to have been on dodgem cars but at least the authorities now had someone they could track through the fair.

She left Peter and his mother and sat down at the main desk to get on to the details of the contact they now had at infectious diseases control.

'We'll send someone to talk to Peter and his mother,' the voice promised. 'It will give us two visits to compare—we haven't liked to disturb Rosa's family at this time. And we'll have to publicise this now. Be ready for a few journalists, TV cameras, et cetera.'

'My boss can do that,' Sam said firmly, and the woman laughed.

'If you can get Andy Wilkie to front the cameras, you're a better woman than I am,' she said.

'No way—no, never!' Andy told Sam very firmly when she came to his office at the end of her shift to tell him journalists would be on their way.

'But why not?' Sam asked, frowning at him, the spark that had flared between them earlier tamped down now under the pressure of work.

'I just don't do it!' he said bluntly. 'This is a small regional hospital, and once the press latch onto someone they can use as an "expert" or "hospital spokesperson—"' he put the words in inverted commas with his fingers '—they never let him or her go.'

He paused then spread out his hands.

'Have you ever done it? They put powder all over your face and shine bright lights into your eyes so you look like a startled rabbit. Only in my case I look like a very tall, gangly, startled rabbit. Never! The Administrator can do it. He can get all the info he needs off the computer, and he'll handle the press far better than I would.'

But still Sam frowned, apparently not at all placated by his flood of words.

'What?' he asked, and now she smiled.

'You must have done it at some time,' she pointed out, 'to know you look like a very tall, startled rabbit.'

'I did it when Nick died,' he said, voice flat and cold, obviously still distressed by the memory. 'I was there at the hospital that day. Some people knew I was his friend and sicced a reporter onto me.'

Holy cow! What had he done, blurting that out?

He didn't need to see Sam's stricken face to realise that, just like that, he'd spread all the horror of the past on his desk in front of her—in front of them both—because she'd know immediately why he'd been at the hospital that day. He'd been there to yell at her!

'Shit!' he said, and buried his face in his hands. 'I'm sorry, Sam, so sorry.'

But sorry was too late. She'd been transported as rapidly as he had back to that dreadful day, and now the tentative attraction that had flared between them, piping hot only a few hours earlier, had vanished beneath the weight of old, and very cold, memories.

'I understand,' she finally said, in a voice devoid of feeling. 'I'm sure they'll find someone else to do it.' And with that she was gone.

This relationship was never going to work.

No matter how he felt about Sam, the past would always be there, hovering in the background, ready to leap out and bite them at the most unexpected moments.

Sam left work feeling unsettled and anxious. She'd thrust Andy back into those memories with her teasing him about being on TV, but did that mean…

You are over Nick, she told herself firmly. You won't ever forget him, the great times with Nick and the love she'd had for him, but it was time to move on.

And given the effect Andy was having on her, surely he was the man to move on with?

For now, at least.

Although those last two words made her stomach ache. If she wanted even just for now, she somehow had to show Andy that everything was all right between them.

Somehow…

* * *

Tom Carey was the first man she'd seen in a suit since her arrival—very smooth and efficient, rattling off numbers she really didn't understand, or want to learn about.

But she'd already spotted the car she wanted, a vivid yellow, compact four-wheel drive tucked into a back corner of the showroom.

'But will you need a four-wheel drive? Wouldn't a nice sedan—a small one—suit you better?'

'Not if I'm going to explore the places around Port on my days off,' she told him, pleased the name the locals used had come easily to her lips. 'I saw from up on the lighthouse hill that the country begins quickly on the outskirts of town, and while I don't intend to do any dangerous off-road driving, I'll be more comfortable in something that doesn't hate country roads.'

Tom took her across to look at the interior of the car, though she assured him she didn't need to see the engine as she had no idea what it was supposed to look like.

'Want to take it for a spin?' Tom asked, and she smiled and nodded.

It was a glorious car to drive, not too high

off the ground but high enough to see over many of the cars around her.

'I love it,' she told Tom, then realised that probably wasn't a good bargaining point, but it already had its price written on the back window, and with new cars she wouldn't have a lot of bargaining power, but she tried anyway.

'Can I get the window tinting included in the price?' she asked, and Tom agreed without any argument so she guessed the company allowed for that in its profit margin.

Fifteen minutes of paperwork later, the car insured and registered, she drove out of the dealership filled with the joy and pride of ownership.

Remembering the uneasiness between her and Andy before she'd left the hospital, she drove to the shopping centre and picked up all she'd need to cook a decent meal for the two of them, deciding on roast lamb because she knew people living alone rarely bothered with a roast dinner.

The residual chill she'd felt in Andy's office remained with her, but it hadn't completely doused the heat that had flared between them earlier, and if she wanted to retrieve that—wanted to be with Andy, even just for now—she had to make things right between them again.

Rod had given her a remote to access the garage and she drove in proudly, finding the double space for Unit One and parking her car beside what was presumably Rod's.

Would Andy guess it was hers when he drove in past it?

She smiled at the thought then bundled her groceries out of the car and up in the elevator to Andy's floor, pleased she still had his keys.

But even as she marinated the roast in rosemary and lemon, and prepared the vegetables so everything was ready to go into the oven when he returned home, misgivings swirled in her stomach and she was tempted to open the bottle of quality shiraz she'd bought and have a drink to settle her nerves.

Better to go downstairs for a shower and change of clothes, she decided, but as she reached the elevator, it stopped and Andy stepped out.

He took her in his arms and held her close.

'I was so sure I'd ruined everything, bringing up the past like that. I just didn't realise what I was saying. I was so adamant about not appearing on television again I wasn't thinking.'

He nuzzled his lips against her neck, then kissed her lips, the kiss deepening as the charge she'd felt this morning returned.

'I was just going down for a shower,' she murmured weakly.

'I need one too,' he told her, so somehow it was inevitable they both ended up in his shower, exploring each other with touch and kisses, less frantic this time, prolonging their pleasure until satisfaction could wait no longer, and they joined beneath the running water, gloriously slick, and cool, intensifying the experience.

'Well, that's going to make dinner a little late,' she said, smiling at him as she towelled her hair dry, marvelling at the sight of him naked, his body lithe yet muscular from his swimming and surfing. 'And I need to get clean clothes from my room but don't want to go down there wrapped in a towel.'

He slipped out of the bathroom, returning with a T-shirt with a large dog on the front of it and a pair of his boxers.

'They've an elastic waist so should stay up on you, although maybe not for long,' he teased, his blue eyes glinting with mischief.

But Sam had a dinner to prepare, so she put on the offered clothes and headed for the kitchen, turned on the oven, and when it had heated put the meat and vegetables into it.

'And wine, too?' Andy said, when he returned, similarly attired in a baggy shirt and boxers, explaining when she raised her eyebrows, 'I thought it'd be nice to match.'

He opened the wine and poured two glasses, kissing her lightly on the lips as he handed one to her.

'Let's sit outside,' she said, and headed for the balcony, quite sure where kisses would lead if they stayed in the kitchen.

'I didn't think you'd come,' he said, as they raised their glasses in a toast. 'But you'll be pleased to know I did the interview. I decided I'd let Nick's death colour my life for far too long. I knew I'd hurt you when I brought the whole darned thing up again this morning, so I did my powdered, startled rabbit thing not long after you left. If you want to see it, we'll probably catch it on the late local news.'

She smiled at him.

'If we happen to be around to catch the late local news!'

Sam felt herself blush as she said it. That was surely flirting, and she'd never flirted much—certainly not with Nick, who could so easily take something the wrong way. But Andy winked at her, and she knew everything was going to be all right.

Andy looked out over the ocean, dark now as the moon hadn't yet shown itself. He felt at peace, and knew it was to do with the woman sitting beside him.

Fate had brought this woman back into his life, and now she was here, with him—and even if it *was* just for now, he could be content with it—just for now, anyway...

He understood some of her reservations about relationships, he'd known Nick well enough to know he wouldn't have wanted to work with him. With Nick, everything had to be a contest, with him as the winner, and throughout their friendship, from childhood on, Andy had been content with that.

Winning had never seemed important to him.

Being the best he could—that was something else—but coming second, or even thirty-first, had never bothered him.

And then there were the disasters of his own relationships, failures that had led him to wonder if they were worth the investment he'd put into them; that had led him to step back from too much commitment to anyone.

'Want to share?' Sam asked, and he was startled out of his thoughts.

'Share what?' he said, aware he certainly didn't want to share those particular thoughts, especially not with Sam.

'The myriad thoughts that were chasing across your face—and not all of them good, I suspect.'

He shrugged the words away. 'Just random things floating past, nothing deep and meaningful,' he said. 'I suppose just sitting here with you is enough for me at the moment.'

He smiled at her, sitting with her feet up on the railing of his balcony, her long legs sending a frisson of excitement through him.

'Do you want me to do anything about the dinner—turn something over in the oven, get the cutlery?'

'Just sit and relax,' she said, sipping at her drink. 'And after dinner, if you like, I'll take you for a drive in my new car.'

'You bought a car? Why didn't you say? We could have gone straight down and looked at it.'

'Yes?' she teased, and he had to laugh, but her lack of excitement over such a purchase bemused him. Buying a new car, for him, was right up there with surfing big waves as far as excitement went.

But Sam?

He studied her for a moment, saw her in profile as she watched the moon put in its appearance over the ocean. She was different, this woman. He sensed she had an inner calmness of spirit that meant she could cope with whatever life threw at her. Someone at ease with herself.

Yes, she'd been upset about Rosa, but in no way had it affected her work, or her capacity to empathise with all the other patients and their families, all of whom he knew, even after a week or two, liked and trusted her implicitly.

If he'd been the peevish type, he might have resented her easy popularity—the way nurses would turn to her, parents seek her out—but instead he was proud, not only because he'd appointed her but because she was Sam, and he was happy for her.

Sam sipped her drink, delighting in the peace and quiet of the early evening, happy she could sit like this with Andy, not having to talk, or plan, or, in fact, do anything much.

Shortly she'd have to get up and check on their dinner, but right now all she had to do was sit, comfortable in his presence, relishing his closeness—the feeling of a bond between them that worked without words.

'Sure I can't do anything for you in the kitchen?' he asked and she turned to smile at him, shaking her head.

'Starving, are you?' she teased. 'You can't hurry a roast dinner. I'll take care of it, but we can sit a while longer.'

She paused, remembering the bad moments they'd had earlier in the day, *and* the outcome when he'd arrived home.

This could work, but being with Andy, enjoying the physical side of things, could she let it go when the 'just for now' ended?

She rather doubted it, so with a less content feeling she lowered her legs and headed for the kitchen to pull the lamb out of the oven and wrap it in foil to let it rest, then called Andy, asking him to set the table while she served up.

Which involved coming into the kitchen to get the cutlery and, it appeared, seizing her by the waist and waltzing her around the kitchen island, before releasing her to get on with her job.

But that carefree impulse had left her smiling and wondering again if 'just for now' *would* be enough.

The drive was forgotten as the meal became an erotic feast, feeding titbits to each other, feet tangling beneath the table, hands touching, stroking, the meal in the end only three-quarters eaten as the need grew too great and they moved to the bedroom to pursue the by now red-hot attraction.

Sam woke at three and slid out of the bed, careful not to wake Andy. She pulled on yesterday's clothes to make her way down to her own small living space, showered and slipped into bed. She'd get a couple of hours' good sleep before her alarm told her the new day was waiting for her.

Andy wasn't surprised to find Sam gone when he awoke the next morning. Her work shift began at seven and he'd slept until close to eight. But as he touched the cold sheets beside him, he wished she was still there.

Not for sex, although that would have been nice—but just for company. And with nearly two hours before *he* had to be at work, he could afford to lie here for a while and think about her.

He felt comfortable with Sam—talking to her, being with her, even knowing she was close by when they were on the ward.

And somehow, to him, he decided, that was nearly as good as the sex—though it was great sex—something you couldn't really say about most new relationships—well, in his case anyway.

To get his mind off that particular subject, he ran through the patients on the ward, mentally checking where they all were in their treatment. Grant was a worry. X-rays and scans of his head had revealed little damage to his brain—no swelling, no obvious injuries at all, and although the anaesthetist had reversed the anaesthetic he'd been given to keep him calm for a few days, he'd remained unresponsive.

A neurosurgeon was due to visit him today, and Andy closed his eyes briefly, praying there was nothing the other specialists had missed.

And Jake's rash—still no answer to that.

He drifted back to sleep…

Colin Forbes had appeared as Sam was finishing her first round, checking on any changes to patients' statuses during the night, noting down any problems or anomalies that would require more attention later.

But right now there was a visiting neurologist standing at the monitor desk, going through Grant's file.

'He was alert immediately after the accident?' he asked, when Sam had introduced herself.

'Alert and responding to questions the ambos put to him,' Sam confirmed. 'It was because of the extent of his physical injuries that the surgeons who patched him up decided to put him into an induced coma for a few days, to allow the healing process to begin.'

'And they reversed it, when?'

'Yesterday, late afternoon.'

'And no change?'

'None!' Sam told him, drawing a vacant monitor towards her and pulling up Grant's scans and X-rays.

'Did they do an MRI?' Colin asked, and Sam shook her head.

'Get one done now and ask Radiography to copy to me. Now let's see the boy.'

Sam spoke to the nurse about organising someone to take Grant down to Radiography, then led the specialist to Grant's room, where his mother was reading to the unresponsive boy.

'Good stuff!' Colin told her, then introduced himself. 'The more stimulation a coma patient has the better,' he said, before adding, 'although plenty dispute that. But you keep it up, touch him, talk to him, let him smell things and feel things. It can't do any harm, and who knows what will help.'

Grant's mother happily agreed, saying to Sam as Colin left the room, 'What a lovely man!'

And indeed he was. Sam totally agreed with his notions about providing stimulation for coma patients.

But little Jake was her main problem, his rash far worse. She'd wondered if it could be measles, however unlikely that would be given the child's isolation, but she did return to his bedside to open his mouth, trying to find tell-tale spots among the ulcers the chemo had caused, which was impossible.

Aware he'd been home before the bone-marrow transplant, she wondered if he might have been taken to the fair for a treat.

'Oh, no—no way!' Mrs Wilson responded. 'We kept him well away from any other children and definitely away from crowds. We wanted him as well as possible for the transplant.'

Sam examined him gently, aware he was in a world of misery right now.

The rash was confined to his torso, which really ruled out the wild supposition of measles, the rash usually starting from the face down.

'Could the donor have had some infection?' Mrs Collins asked, but Sam shook her head.

'The donor cells are tested, and then treated to ensure they're totally clear of any infection. But for some reason he's just reacted badly to the transfusion.'

'But on the upside,' a voice behind her said, and this time Andy had come into the room without shivers running up or down her spine, 'it might just be a rash and it will clear up in a couple of days.'

Mrs Collins smiled at him, and Sam wondered at the ease with which Andy could reassure both patients and their families.

They left Jake's room together, Sam explaining the neurologist's visit and his wanting an MRI for Grant.

Andy frowned, and shook his head.

'Surely they'd have picked up anything

when they did that in the ED before he was operated on,' he said.

'Unless there was a small bleed, and it's just continued to bleed. He's not on anti-coagulants—I checked what the surgeons had ordered, but—'

'You're right—a small bleed could have been missed,' Andy finished for her.

And, as if summoned by their thoughts, two uniformed police officers appeared.

'Grant Williams. We were told he'd be conscious again today,' one of them said.

'Might have been but even if he was, he wouldn't be in any fit state to answer questions,' Sam told the two men. 'He's badly injured, and he's still in a coma, but you must realise that even when he comes out of it, he'll be sleepy and confused.'

'That right?' one of them asked, turning to Andy as if he needed a male viewpoint on the situation.

'Dr Reilly is in charge of the patient, so she should know,' he said, and Sam felt her pique at the policeman's question subside.

The two men left, and she turned to thank Andy for his support, but he just grinned at her.

'Actually, I did it to save that poor fellow

from one of your pithy set-downs. I could see the colour rising in your face.'

'Wretch!' she muttered at him, then added, 'But I *am* worried about Grant—worried we've missed something important.'

'Let's wait for the MRI and the neurologist's report before we start worrying. The kid's had a rough few days—he needs time as much as anything else.'

A nurse appeared at that moment with a request from the ED, for someone to see a child with status epilepticus.

'I'll go down,' Andy said, but Sam was already on her way.

'You're not on duty for another two hours,' she reminded him, although inside she was rather hoping he'd come in early because he wanted to see her, maybe even brush against her—as she'd wanted to do with him.

Mind on job, she scolded herself as she arrived on the ground floor, though the thoughts she'd just dismissed did make her wonder again whether relationships between close colleagues were a good idea.

The child, Ahmed, was four years old, Sam read from his paper file as the ED doctor explained.

'Suffers from epilepsy but usually controlled by drugs. Mother gave oral dose of a benzodiazepine, and the ambos established an IV line and gave a second dose. We have a breathing tube in place, blood sugar is low, so we gave a bolus of glucose IV but he's still—well, you can see...'

The little boy was stiff, but his limbs were twitching and his little body twisting.

'We'll admit him,' Sam said, aware they might have to begin second-level drugs, and do further blood and neurological tests. She was pleased to see the neurologist who'd been visiting Grant was listed as the child's regular specialist. Perhaps he was still in the hospital or had rooms nearby.

Colin Forbes was not only in the hospital, but was in the PICU, at the monitor desk, reading a report on Grant from Radiography.

'Look at this,' he said to Sam, turning a monitor so she could see the screen. 'Here!' he said, using a pen to point to a darker mass of matter towards the back of the skull. 'Poor lad was hit so hard by that damn vehicle he had a contra coup injury to the left side at the back of his brain—just a small contusion but it has bled. From his injuries, we know the car hit him on the right side, and his brain must have jolted forward then back against his skull. It wouldn't have been picked up earlier because it wasn't bleeding directly after the accident, then he went up to surgery and it was missed.'

'Would it be causing his lack of response to the reversal of the coma?' Sam asked, but Dr Forbes shrugged.

'Possibly. A case of delayed concussion maybe—that's always possible. But let's just wait and see. It could resolve itself in a day or two.'

Not something Sam wanted to say to the parents, but she knew the specialist was right.

She told him about Ahmed, who should have arrived in the unit by now, and led the way to the room that had been allotted to him. Sam explained the treatment he'd received from the onset of the seizure, and to her surprise he asked, 'And what would you use next?'

'I suggested downstairs they use a second-line anti-epileptic drug like phenytoin, and if that doesn't work by the time they get him transferred, paraldehyde diluted with point nine percent saline.'

He smiled at her. 'You really don't need me, but as Ahmed is one of my patients, I'll definitely see him. I'd like to speak to his mother about the circumstances around the seizure—whether it was brought on by anything, or if the severity of his seizures has been increasing.'

Ahmed was settled in a bed, an ECG connected to his frail chest, the nurse checking the IV line hadn't kinked during the transfer.

Sam checked the file and saw that phenytoin had been administered in the ED more than five minutes ago, and although Ahmed's body seemed less rigid, the twitching continued.

'Go ahead with paraldehyde,' Colin told her, and keep me posted on his progress.'

CHAPTER EIGHT

AND SO THE days progressed, some patients leaving, new ones arriving, but the small core of seriously ill children remaining with them. Grant had regained consciousness but remained in the PICU because of the severity of his injuries and Colin Forbes's desire to keep an eye on his head injury.

But Jake was causing the most concern, the source of his rash still unidentified, although as yet he was showing no sign of rejecting the transfusion of stem cells he'd received. However, far from improving, he remained limp and listless.

Sam had gone from a week of early shifts to six days of night shifts so she'd seen far less of Andy, grabbing a meal together occasionally if he was home from work before she left for her shift.

She'd finished her final night shift and was

looking forward to a full day's sleep, possibly two or three, and sat in her office, writing up some notes. She'd visit Jake before she left, his condition still the main source of concern in the unit.

But as she came out into the airlock room to disrobe, there was Andy, looking so great even robed in white paper that her heart flipped.

'How's our boy?' he asked, although his eyes said other things. Things that made her blush.

She pulled off her mask to smile properly at him, and was untying her gown when she started to feel sick. She ripped off her gown and raced out of the room, still wearing her booties and gloves, heading post haste for the staff lounge and its bathrooms.

Flushed with heat, she knelt by the lavatory, throwing up everything she'd snacked on during the night.

Then, clammy, and still feeling distinctly wonky, she sat back on the floor. She was aware she had to get up, wash out her mouth, wash her face and hands, and generally sort herself out, but she was unable, for the moment, to move.

Snacking on night shift was normal,

mainly because the time seemed all wrong for eating a large meal, but what had she eaten that could do this to her? A couple of cups of tea with biscuits, coffee at some stage, and a sandwich from the machine in the corridor. She couldn't even remember what had been in it, but that seemed the most likely culprit.

Hauling herself to her feet, she made her way out to the washroom to clean herself up and remove her gloves and booties, dumping them in the disposal bin.

Andy was waiting outside when she opened the door.

'Are you all right?' he asked, concern clouding his features.

'Fine now,' she said, 'but I must have eaten something that disagreed with me.'

'Or you've a virus of some kind. Maybe even something you brought back from South-East Asia. You'll have to go home, Sam,' he said. 'I can't risk you being here, maybe passing on something contagious to the children.'

'I *am* going home,' she reminded him. 'End of night shift, four days off, remember, but I doubt it's some bug I picked up before

I came—just too long ago. It's something I ate. I'll be fine once I've had a sleep.'

He stepped towards her and she knew he wanted to hold her as much as she wanted to be held—not a done thing in a staff common room.

'I'll call in and see you when I get off,' he said, reaching out and touching her lightly on the shoulder. 'For now, go home and rest— we'll talk later,' he said quietly, then turned away, leaving Sam feeling weak and sick and badly in need of a hug that just hadn't come.

Sorry she hadn't driven her new car to work, Sam trudged home, feeling quite well now but upset that she hadn't finished the handover and had let the team down—let Andy down!

She'd get her car and go to a pathology lab in town, ask for all the tests they could think of for possible overseas viral or bacterial complaints. But not today—today she'd sleep...

By the following morning, she felt so well she knew it couldn't possibly be anything other than something she'd eaten that had disagreed with her. She phoned Andy to explain how well she was, but only midway through the conversation the sick feeling returned, bile rising in her throat, so she said a hasty goodbye and headed for her own small bathroom.

Where, fifteen minutes later, sitting on a different cool, tiled floor, her brain began to work again, and she had to close her mind against the answer it had reached.

Surely not?

It couldn't be!

But it had been over two weeks since Rosa's death, and she knew from the last time that a pregnancy was dated from the date of the last period, and that morning sickness could begin within three to four weeks of that date.

Which, to her, last time, had seemed totally unreasonable!

But this time?

It was impossible!

How could she possibly be pregnant after one night of grief-driven lust?

True, there'd been more nights together since, but she'd gone onto the Pill, and Andy had been scrupulous in using protection until it was well into her system.

So, what the hell was Andy going to think?

She went cold all over, dreading a repeat

of the storm her previous pregnancy had caused—remembering the tragedy that it had led to. Not that she had long to find out what Andy thought...

Deciding the best thing to do would be to cook him dinner that evening, and as they relaxed over fine food she'd—well, probably blurt it out!

She'd leave a note on her door that she was up in his apartment, and—

Stop!

First and foremost was the decision *she* had to make.

How did *she* feel?

What did *she* want?

The first was easy—she was delighted at the thought—and the answer lay in the second question—a baby.

She'd already lost one baby and although it had been barely the size of a fist, her arms had ached for it.

This baby she would keep.

And, yes, it would be difficult as she still wanted to work—would *have* to work in order to provide a decent life for herself and her child.

And, really, apart from wanting to keep working, she owed it to Andy, who'd employed her, to stay on. But working women had options these days, and a hospital as new as Port's would almost certainly have a crèche and day-care centre tucked away somewhere in its building.

So, that was *her* decisions made.

In, what, in all of three minutes?

You really gave this a lot of thought, Sam!

But chiding herself didn't stop the secret glee she clutched inside her, ignoring all she knew about the uncertainties tied to the first months of any pregnancy.

It would be the start of her family, her mum's longed-for grandchild. She hugged herself in sheer delight...

Her happy secret kept her going all day as she shopped and prepared a meal for herself and Andy, but about the time he was due to arrive home it occurred to her that Andy would be entitled to some say in this matter. After all, it would be his baby too...

Although if he didn't want a baby, wasn't ready, or thought they should be married but didn't fancy that idea, she'd be quite happy to raise the baby on her own.

All Andy had to decide was whether he'd like to take an interest in it—or even accept a fatherhood role—be part of its life for ever.

The glow was fading slightly, especially now she'd *really* considered Andy and his reaction. He might be horrified.

Probably would be horrified…

She had to stop thinking about it, and definitely stop projecting all the possible reactions Andy might have to hear the news before she became too worried about it that telling him would be impossible.

She *did* blurt it out in the end, but at least not until they'd eaten, and she'd stacked their dirty plates and cutlery in the dishwasher and left the kitchen sparkling clean. Eventually she'd joined him on the balcony, a glass of sparkling mineral water in her hand.

He'd taken her hand to draw her closer but she'd resisted, thinking it best not to be too close, actually edging her chair a little further away.

All the things she'd been going to say, all the ways of telling him she'd practised, vanished in a split second as she clutched her water more tightly in her hand and came out with an abrupt, 'I'm pregnant!'

And apart from seeing his face freeze in reaction, she took no further notice of him as everything else she wanted to say came rushing after those two words.

'I didn't have a virus and this happened last time, the early morning sickness thing, and I'm happy to bring the baby up on my own, or if you want involvement then that's okay too, and I know it will interfere with my work but I'll make sure it interferes as little as possible because I want to keep working and—'

He held up his hand like a policeman, signalling her to stop, and as her flow of words did stop he said, 'What last time? And how come you get to say if my involvement is okay or not? And, anyway, we need to talk about this, Sam!' He paused, then added, 'Seriously talk, Sam.'

Feeling completely deflated, Sam waited, and when he said nothing else, anxiety began to grow where the joy had once been. And well aware of how quickly anxiety could lead to anger, she had to prod.

'So talk,' she said, pleased her voice didn't shake too much as she spoke.

He squeezed the fingers of the hand she was surprised to find he still held.

'This is hard,' he began, 'but, seriously, Sam, you shouldn't have this baby.'

Sam stared at him in total shock. She'd been prepared for him not wanting involvement, even for him to be angry at the place they'd landed in, but for his first reaction to be a termination, without any discussion or reasoning, that blew her mind.

And took her right back to three years ago when Nick had made a similar pronouncement, only his had been a blunt, 'Get rid of it!'

And ten minutes later he'd been dead.

Red mist gathered in her head and she knew she had to leave, snatching back her hand and rushing off the balcony, through the living room and out the front door, only vaguely aware of Andy saying something to her, getting up to follow her and knocking over his chair on the way.

But she was gone, racing down the fire stairs rather than waiting for the lift, needing to get back into the small space that was her own, where she could hold herself and breathe and remember the excitement she'd been feeling all day long.

Andy let her go.

She had another three days off then a late

shift. Hopefully she'd feel well enough to keep working.

Oh, for heaven's sake, why the hell are you thinking about Sam's work hours and shifts? You have to see her, tell her, explain, sort things out.

This wasn't the end of the world.

Then something she'd said—something else—echoed in his bemused brain.

'This happened last time!'

When had she been pregnant before?

Not by Nick, surely, given Nick's steely determination that they both finish their specialty courses before they even thought about a family.

And, slowly, a glimmer of light appeared. She'd said she probably *had* caused the accident—that they'd been arguing—and knowing Nick, nothing would have made him angrier than an announcement by Sam that she was pregnant…

He sighed, remembering the harsh words he'd flung at her at a time when her whole world must have been crashing down around her—when the pain of loss would have been crushing her usually indomitable spirit.

But that was the past, and right now he had problems of his own to solve.

Sam had been happy, her face aglow as she'd announced her pregnancy, and he'd said exactly the worst possible thing.

But how to explain?

How to tell her that genetic testing only identified eighty-five to ninety percent of carriers, which was great, of course, but oh hell and damnation, he'd already been through all this before, the first time after his engagement, but the second time he'd explained first.

And neither of those women, who had professed to loving him deeply and wholly, had wanted to go ahead with a marriage to him.

Could he watch Sam walk away if he told her—*when* he told her?

Especially now, when he'd known this 'just for now' talk was nonsense and he wanted her—loved her—more than anything else in his life. Probably had done for years.

He closed his eyes to the beauty around him and tried to think, but his mind refused to work, blocked by fear of losing Sam.

He had to see her, talk to her, explain…

Sam lay on her bed and stared at the ceiling, her hands cradling her stomach, although it had yet to produce the slightest of bumps.

Stupid, that's what she'd been, reacting like that—like a spoilt child told she couldn't have what she wanted.

She should go back.

Andy must have had a reason for saying what he had.

Surely he did!

But memories of that other time cut too deep—the bitterness, the implacability of Nick's attitude, the anger then the crash—made her dread the conversation that she knew, only too well, she'd have to have with Andy sometime.

But not tonight. Tonight she was far too irrational; the two rejections somehow melding into one.

She had another three days off. She'd sleep and read, and maybe go to the beach or drive around the town, and tomorrow night—surely by tomorrow night—she'd be able to talk sensibly and calmly to Andy, explain how she felt, assure him she could do it on her own, that he needn't be involved.

She shook her head.

Andy *not* be involved?

She'd seen enough of him around the ward to know he'd make a fantastic father. So maybe it was her? Maybe she was okay 'just for now' but not for long term, as a mother of his children.

Dear heaven, she had to stop thinking like this, stop her mind going round and round in circles. She should pick up a book and lose herself in it until she fell asleep. She'd been on night duty, she was tired…

She had a shower, thinking it would soothe her—help her sleep—but Andy's words were a constant echo in her head—*Really, Sam, you shouldn't have this baby…*

Rod woke her with a soft tapping at the door, calling her name. Face crumpled from sleep, hair like a haystack from her tossing and turning all night, she went to it, opening it a crack.

'Andy is here. He wants to see you, just for a minute, before he goes to work.'

Rod was looking anxiously at her and a sideways glance at her mirrored wardrobe doors told her just how bad she *did* look.

Then the nausea came—she'd slept late and not eaten—and she had to flee, managing a garbled, 'Sorry,' to Rod as she shut the door in his face and rushed to the bathroom.

And as she sat on a cool, tiled floor yet again, her stomach empty and the muscles around it complaining, she wondered if Andy was right.

Maybe she *shouldn't* have this baby?

But the mere word 'baby' made her smile, and she hugged her body and told herself she'd manage, get through this, and make a life for herself and her child.

The text was there when she awoke the second time.

I've booked a table for dinner at the Lighthouse Restaurant for tonight at eight. Bring a warm wrap so we can sit outside and talk. I'll knock on Rod's door about seven forty-five. Please let me know.

They *did* need to talk, but there was something very remote about the text—something detached—one colleague to another, rather than a text between lovers.

Not that love had ever been mentioned, although now Sam thought about *that* she felt distinctly unhappy. As if somewhere in the just-for-now scenario, love had entered the picture.

On her side, anyway.

So a cool, unemotional, colleague-type text made her heart ache.

But love wasn't the issue right now, she reminded herself. This was about the baby— someone she could love unreservedly!

She'd bought fresh bread the previous day and was trialling dry toast and a cup of tea for breakfast, hoping it would quell the nausea so her work days wouldn't be disrupted.

And if it worked, she'd head for the beach this morning, slathering on sunscreen and not staying long—just time for a swim and a short sunbake to dry off.

Andy stared at his phone. Sam had replied to his text, but somehow the single word— Okay—made him feel worse than no reply.

No, he couldn't feel worse, but what the hell did Okay tell him? Abso-bloody-lutely nothing, that was what!

Somehow he made it through the day, pleased to see improvement in most of his patients, although some of the new admissions were causing problems, including a fourth measles case.

Given the high percentage of children who *did* receive all their immunisations, he hated to think how many there would have been if more parents had opted out.

But at least the people at Infectious Diseases had isolated the carrier now, an older man who'd fallen ill in Port, but unfortunately he hadn't been ill enough to take to his bed and keep away from the general population.

'It was just a cold and a sore throat,' he'd told his interviewer. 'Yes, maybe a bit of a rash, but I didn't connect the two. You can brush against something, get a rash anywhere!'

It was the only real diversion in a long work day, which finally ended with a Heads of Department meeting that dragged on and on.

He'd finally stood up, apologising but saying he had to leave for another appointment, surprising not a few of the other department heads, who all assumed he had no life outside the hospital.

Not that they'd been wrong about that—not until recently, anyway…

Now, as he drove home—having driven to work to avoid being late—his gut was clenching and his nausea was probably rivalling Sam's morning sickness. Just thinking those two words filled him with so much confusion he had to shut down his wretched imagination and concentrate on practical matters, like what shirt to wear.

Did it matter?

Not one jot, he suspected, but he had to think about something.

Sam had been waiting by the door and opened it when Andy knocked.

Her mind had played out so many scenarios of this moment, most of them as formal as his text, so she was totally undone when he opened his arms and drew her close, murmuring, 'Oh, my love, I'm so sorry!'

Hugging her to him, rocking her in his arms, just holding her.

'This *is* the main entry foyer and a public space,' a voice behind Andy said, and they broke apart, Sam glaring at Rod's huge smile and furious with herself for blushing.

Grabbing hold of Andy's hand, she said, 'Come on, let's go!' and all but dragged him out the front door.

Andy's car was sitting in one of the drop-off, pick-up bays.

'I thought we'd walk,' she said, embarrassed now by her reaction to Rod's tease.

'Driving, we can talk,' Andy said, turning so he could take both her hands in his. 'And we *do* need to talk.'

She looked up into his anxious blue eyes.

'It's not the baby, Sam. There's nothing I'd like more,' he said quietly, then he opened the car door for her, and she slid into the seat.

'But there's something I need to tell you,' he added, as he joined her in the car.

Sam waited, her anxiety, which had vanished in Andy's warm hug, slowly squirming its way inside her once again.

They drove up to the lighthouse, the moon sparkling on the ocean below, the night picture perfect. As was the restaurant, with elegant starched white tablecloths and gleaming silver and glassware, while the outside deck looked north along the coastline and the ocean, occasional clusters of lights suggesting small beachside hamlets.

But it wasn't until they each had glasses of sparkling mineral water in their hands, and the waiter had departed with their orders, that Andy broke the tension that had been gathering between them.

'It's a genetic thing,' he said, and she knew she'd frowned because he held up his hand to stop her questions. 'I'm a carrier for cystic fibrosis. I had a younger sister who had it, so I was tested as well. It means you will need to be tested because most carriers have no idea they are carrying it, unless they've been impacted by a relative with the disease.'

'And you were?' she asked, thinking of very sick children with CF that she'd cared for in the past. 'You *had* a sister? She died?'

She saw the sadness in his eyes, but he waved her questions away, needing, she guessed, to get said what he wanted to tell her.

'Unfortunately testing only reveals eighty-five to ninety percent of carriers. There are rare mutations that aren't revealed.'

He sounded so stressed she reached out and took his hand, aware that this was very difficult for him, while her own mind whirled through possible consequences. Survival rates for cystic fibrosis were much better these days, and if a sufferer could get a heart-lung transplant they had a good chance of leading a good life.

But it was a condition that limited a child's life enormously, and not something she would ever want to see a child of hers go through.

'So, I get tested to see if I'm a carrier,' she

said, 'and hope I'm not one, for a start. I guess there's nothing we can do about the chances of my being one of the five to ten percent who might have it but don't get picked up?'

She could hear the hesitation in her voice and knew how hard it was for him to tell her this.

Andy nodded. 'Yes, but in case you are in that group, we should test the foetus too,' he said. 'CVS testing at ten to twelve weeks or amniocentesis at sixteen to twenty weeks, although even if we are both carriers there's only a one in four chance the baby would have it.'

Sam could only stare at him, aware he'd lived with this for most of his life so the facts and figures rolled off his tongue.

CVS—chorionic villus sampling—was where a small number of cells were taken from the placenta close to where it attached to the uterus. Her hand went automatically to her belly, as if she could hold the baby safe from this intrusion.

'Did your parents know?' she asked, wondering if she'd be willing to take the chance of having children if something like this could occur.

Andy shook his head. 'As far back as either of their parents or grandparents were concerned, no one remembered a child who was seriously ill from birth.'

He paused, then added, 'Not that that mattered. They had Sarah and she was a blessing to our family. She was so funny and smart, Sam, and so unconcerned about the difficulties she faced every day.'

He paused.

'We loved her,' he said simply, but his voice was tight, and Sam reached out to hold his hand. Some other time they'd talk more about Sarah, but for now she had to concentrate on her child—their child...

She'd get tested for CF, and if she wasn't found to be a carrier, there was only a minimal chance of her being one of the rare ones, and even if she was... She shuddered at the thought then pushed it away—all the odds were in her favour, although she knew nothing of her father's family, nothing of her father, for that matter.

'If I'm not a carrier then there's no problem,' she said.

'We'd still have to test the baby,' Andy told her. 'Remember the small percentage of people with the rare mutation that testing doesn't reveal.'

Sam sighed and shook her head, unable to take it all in, staring down at the table and fiddling with her cutlery, twirling her knife on the stiffly starched tablecloth.

'Let's wait and see,' she said. 'At the moment it's just all ifs and buts and maybes— all hypothetical. Whatever my test reveals, I'll get the foetus tested and go from there. Okay?'

Andy had to smile at Sam, refusing to get carried away with possibilities, or be concerned over things that might never eventuate. He might mull over it all, and run through dozens of scenarios in his head, but she just got on with things—meeting problems head on. Practical, loving Sam.

Their meals arrived, and as they ate they talked about the food, how good it was, how special to be eating with the ocean right there below them, yet he knew Sam's brain would be working through consequences, and that this was only a temporary lull in the main conversation.

And as the waiter took their plates and left them with a dessert menu, the topic did resume again.

'There's a huge amount of research being

done about CF at the moment,' she said, 'and treatments are improving all the time. Imagine if a heart-lung transplant had been available for your sister, Sarah.'

She was smiling at the thought, and Andy could only shake his head. He'd hit Sam with what must have been quite frightening news and here she was thinking of the positives.

Although… Andy knew she was speaking calmly and rationally, but his mind had snagged back at the testing part of her conversation. Sam's use of the little words 'I' and 'I'll' had rattled him. Surely it should have been 'we' and 'us'…

Did she not want it to be a shared venture—not want to marry him and make a family with this baby and maybe others?

Because she didn't love him?

Or because of the CF thing?

His heart ached, and he longed to ask, but his fear of her answer was greater than his need to know. So he changed the subject.

'You said, when you told me you were pregnant, "that last time" your morning sickness had begun early. When was "that last time", Sam? Surely I'd have known of it?'

CHAPTER NINE

To TELL OR not to tell?

Did it really matter after all this time?

Sam studied the dessert menu as she pondered the questions, not seeing any of the options, just trying to think. Then, aware of the tension growing between them, she lifted her head to meet Andy's eyes.

'That was the cause of the argument,' she said, the words blunt and hard as stones. 'Between Nick and me—when we crashed.'

Another pause, the words that had been held in by locked-away memories caused such pain and guilt she could barely speak. Then, slowly, it came out.

'Nick said a baby would interrupt my career trajectory—and to me it was such a stupid thing to say, especially as I so wanted a family. I blew up.'

She studied Andy's face, seeking understanding—compassion even—but in her emotional state saw nothing.

'I hadn't had a family—not a real one. Just me and Mum. I thought Nick knew how much I wanted children, I'd talked about it often enough.'

Andy nodded, but it was an uncomfortable nod. He'd always known a family hadn't been part of Nick's agenda, although, apparently, Sam, his wife, had not!

But she had a story to tell—a confession to finish.

She took a deep breath, twiddled her dessert spoon, then met Andy's eyes again.

'He said, get rid of it. Those were his first words, then he went on and on about how it would wreck my career and his career, and I lost it, Andy. Said he didn't know me at all—didn't know how much I ached for a family. I was furious with him—I said things I should never have said, things about him having controlled my life for too long. I was so angry—real redhead rage—I was yelling like a madwoman. It was no wonder Nick was speeding.'

'Sam!'

The single word made her blink, and now she *did* see concern and understanding on his face, and as he took her hands in both of his, the hot memories of her anger melted away and she clung to his fingers—a lifeline back to the present…

'You can't keep blaming yourself,' he said, his voice scratchy with emotion. 'I know I was in shock and somehow took that out on you and I'll never forgive myself for that, but you weren't to blame. Yes, the things you said might have upset Nick, but he was a grown man, thirty-five, and reacting by speeding was a stupid thing to do—*his stupid reaction* caused that crash, not your words.'

'But I lost the baby,' Sam said, still trapped in her memories. 'I could have walked away from Nick—divorced him, kept the baby and followed a new career, even though I'd never considered my work as a "career"—never even thought about a bloody career trajectory!'

Andy smiled at her. 'I know that, love,' he said gently, and that one little word, tacked onto a simple reassurance, made her heart leap.

'Dessert?'

She shook her head, hugging the word to her, although she knew it was probably just a casual endearment.

He'd made it very clear he'd taken her in because she was his best friend's widow—love between them had never been mentioned, although she hadn't realised how she'd felt about Andy until...

Well, that had been her reason to move out.

'So, whatever happens, you want to keep this baby?' he said.

Brought back to earth with a thud, she could only shake her head.

'I'll get genetic testing first and let's go from there. CSV sampling will tell us the baby's okay, and after that— Oh, Andy!'

She knew she was probably looking piteously into his eyes, and could hear the plea in her voice, but how the hell did you make that kind of decision? Surely, as a medical practitioner it would be an ethical one, but for her as a person such a very personal one.

'Let's pay the bill and walk,' he said, as she saw the shadows on his face—shadows of the past, reflections of the shadows she'd have had on hers earlier.

'*Two* near marriages?' she probed, as they walked towards the cliff-top in front of the lighthouse, desperately needing to get away from her own problems.

He nodded.

'So tell me,' she said gently.

'The CF thing did raise issues,' he said, sliding his hand out of hers and clasping both hands behind his back, a clear signal to her that this was not a subject he wished to pursue. Because he still felt deeply about the women—or about one of them in particular?

She'd loved Nick, but would have left him in a heartbeat to have the child she'd so longed for. Which kind of answered the question about this baby. Providing she wasn't a carrier, and the baby tested negative for CF, then she'd…

Damn and blast, why did life have to be so difficult?

'Hey, you'll be over the cliff if you don't slow down!'

She should be thinking about Andy, not her own problems, she reminded herself, stopping by the protective railing and looking down.

Andy's voice brought her out of her useless speculation, and she turned back towards him, aware she'd been getting carried away—aware of him.

'There's too much to think about,' she said, walking back and taking his hands in hers as she faced him. 'And I *have* to think about it, Andy.'

'I know, love,' he said, so gently and quietly she thought her heart might break.

She moved closer and put her arms around him, held him—waiting, hoping.

For what?

Words of love?

'Just get the testing done and we'll go from there,' he said, easing her back a little so he could look into her face. But with the moon behind him, his remained in shadow and told her nothing.

They walked back to the car in silence, the magic all around them unnoticed or maybe it had gone completely.

'Just get the testing done, and we'll go from there.'

His words echoed in her head.

Go where? she wanted to ask, but if she proved to be a carrier...

They could have this baby if it tested negative, but other babies—the family she wanted? She could go the IVF route so the fertilised eggs were tested, and only the ones without CF implanted, but...

You are getting far too carried away with yourself You want a family, but Andy has said nothing about it—might not even want to be part of this one.

Just get the test and go from there!

They drove home in silence, both, she imagined, lost in their own thoughts. And as he pulled the car into the underground car park she knew the silence needed to be broken. It had already grown to something far too big between them.

And any bigger?

Well, there'd be no them.

If there *was* a them to begin with.

Her heart ached at the thought. 'Just for now' hadn't really started, and it was over—or all but over—before it had begun.

'Do you know of a good medical practice nearby? I'll need a referral for the test.'

It wasn't the perfect way to break the silence, but at least it was practical. And Andy grasped at it.

'There's one in the main shopping centre in town, the one behind the hospital.'

The silence resumed, but only for an instant.

'I'll come with you,' he said, and she had to smile.

'Andy, it's only a blood test, or maybe a swab from inside my cheek. I could do it myself and send it to a private testing agency but let's not get too carried away.'

He'd stopped the car and opened his door so they had a little light, and she saw the concern on his face—concern that seemed to be easing towards dread.

She took his hand.

'I'll be fine,' she told him. 'It's a lot to think about, but it's pointless getting too far ahead of ourselves with all the what-ifs. Let's just get this first test done and take it from there.'

'If you're sure you don't want me there...'

The hesitant words made her smile.

'Andy, it's a *blood test*!'

He didn't answer, getting out of the car and coming around to open her door, which she would normally have done herself, only she was puzzling over why he was so concerned.

Had the last woman he'd asked to take a test broken his heart?

Refused, and walked away?

Did he still love her?

She slammed the door on the thoughts sprouting in her brain, and took Andy's offered hand so he helped her out of the car, and then he took her in his arms and held her close.

'Kind of put a dampener on the evening,' he said softly into her ear, and the warmth of his breath against her skin had her body stirring. But she knew she had too much thinking to do to be getting more involved with Andy.

Although as his lips moved to the little hollow beneath her chin she wondered just what harm there'd be in going ahead with 'just for now'.

Heaps, you idiot, her head yelled at her. Your heart's already far too involved, don't make it worse,

'We'd better go before Rod appears and tells us it's a public car park,' she said, easing away from him. She fled, aware she'd been rude, hadn't even thanked him for dinner, but right now she needed solitude, and a space she could call her own in which to think.

Andy watched her disappear through the heavy fire door, and realised he had absolutely no idea where he stood with this woman he was pretty sure he loved.

Had loved, certainly, when he and Nick had first met her.

She'd been an intern, rostered onto the ED

for a term, and she'd been so bright, so alive, even on days when she'd worked through the night and stayed on because she was needed.

And he'd stupidly, as it turned out, had his one and only experience of love at first sight. It had been ridiculous, really, as he'd kept telling himself all through Nick's court-ship of her and her starry-eyed wedding to his best mate.

But that was a long time ago, and what he felt now—well, this was certainly different, this was like a deep ache in his gut.

As if he was right back in the past again, in the agony of wanting a woman he couldn't have. Loving her?

He shook his head, aware he didn't want to answer that question even to himself.

He'd loved Annabel, but she'd obviously not loved him enough that she could back away at the first mention of CF, refusing even to consider a genetic test because she'd wanted children and wouldn't risk him as a father.

Which left him where?

Forget it, he told himself. He might not need to think about any of this or make any decisions. The next decision would surely be Sam's.

* * *

The medical centre had an appointment for
her. Port being a holiday centre, they usually
employed extra locums at these times. The
pathology office was next door, so by mid-
day she was done.

The genetic testing of the foetus would
need a specialist, who had offices in the private hospital, where she could also have the
sample taken under ultrasound.

While on a roll, she made an appointment
to see an obstetrician in a couple of weeks,
then, because she'd driven into town, took a
detour home so she could get a feel for the
place and check out the private hospital.

Aware she was getting far too far ahead
of herself but unable to stop herself hoping,
she began to think about options.

If she stayed with the obstetrician through
her pregnancy, she'd probably have her baby
here, although if she stuck with the public
system she'd probably have a group of other
mothers with her all the way and a midwife
she could contact at any time.

And, if anything went wrong—like a premature birth—her baby would end up in the
public system anyway, as they had the best
neonatal facilities.

But she was impressed by the cottagey look of the private hospital—she'd check it out when she had her specialist appointment.

Following no particular route, she drove through suburb after suburb, most of them fairly new, as if the town's expansion into a city had been recent, but she loved the tree-lined streets—the trees still small but promising shade and privacy in the future.

Her phone rang as she climbed out of her car.

Andy!

'How did it go?'

'The blood test was fine, as easy and straightforward as you imagine. No instant results so we just have to wait. But I've made an appointment for an obstetrician to do the CVS, and I drove past the private hospital where he has his offices and through some new and not quite so new suburbs. It seemed from the amount of building that the town developed rapidly.'

'A new hospital, a university, even a big government science establishment, which could, from all the rumours, be developing robots small enough to be inserted into humans to control bad impulses. Or hamburgers made from insects—that's another school of thought. In truth, no one knows but they've a big establishment on the edge of town and every kind of animal imaginable in paddocks around it, leading to a fair few unlikely rumours about interbreeding between species, so who knows?'

'Don't you know anyone working there that you could ask?' Sam said, intrigued by the ideas.

'I do, and they just smile at me so my imagination has even more lurid fantasies.'

Sam laughed. 'More lurid than mind-controlling bots?' she teased.

'Far more lurid.' He laughed, and asked if they could meet up when he finished work.

'I guess so,' Sam said, but she did wonder if she needed a bit of distance between herself and Andy so she could get her head straightened out.

But meeting after work didn't eventuate, Andy being kept late by the admission of a two-year-old who had found small button batteries in a jar and swallowed them, thinking they were candy.

An X-ray showed eight still in the stomach but fortunately revealed none in the oesophagus or windpipe.

'We'll do a small procedure called an endoscopy,' he explained to the parents, aware he wouldn't want to leave the hospital until he knew the child was all right.

But this was how life would be for him and Sam, should they ever manage to get together.

He swore inwardly and continued his explanation to the parents.

'He'll be given light anaesthesia and the surgeon will pass a tube down his throat into his stomach to retrieve the batteries, and also check that there's no damage to the lining of his stomach. He'll be very sleepy after it, but it's not a major procedure for him.'

After settling the parents in the waiting room, with tea and biscuits and magazines in an attempt to take their minds from what was happening, he accompanied the surgeon to Theatre. He'd do the anaesthesia, and that way see what was going on inside his patient.

'I can see eight on the X-ray,' the surgeon said. 'Do we know how many he swallowed?'

'The mother didn't have a clue, but the father thought maybe there could have been ten in the bottle.'

'What on earth were they used for?' the assisting nurse asked, and Andy shook his head as he considered how easily such things happened.

'Apparently, one of the parents' elderly grandfathers lives with them, and he wears hearing aids, but he's always taking the batteries out and leaving them all over the place, so they're gathered up as soon as they're seen and put into the bottle, to be used when he loses another pair.'

'Well, I've got eight,' the surgeon said, and peering at the screen Andy could see eight of the tiny batteries now encased in a tiny bag.

'I'll bring them out, but some could have gone further into his digestive tract, so the parents should watch for more appearing in his stools.'

He paused before adding, 'I'd be happier if we'd known the exact number.'

'None appeared in the digestive tract in the X-ray,' Andy reminded him, although they both knew with the folds within the small intestine something so small would appear as little more than a tiny blip.

'We'll just have to hope for the best,' he added, wondering if hoping for the best was all you could do with your own children in many situations.

He was beginning to think like Sam, worrying about possible accidents and illnesses to possible children.

Because now there was a child?

The thought excited him to the extent he smiled, although he knew there was still a long way to go before he and Sam could explore their options further as far as the current possibility went.

He and Sam?

Would there ever be an Andy and Sam?

'All done,' the surgeon said. 'You should keep him up in the PICU for twenty-four hours, but I couldn't see any obvious damage to the lining of his stomach so he should be fine.'

Andy stayed with the boy in Recovery, wanting to assure himself he really *was* all right. And possibly as an excuse not to go home just yet.

He had to talk to Sam—to talk about things other than CF—but he was fairly sure that, at the moment, it was in the forefront of her mind, and the admissions of love he'd like to make to her would go unheard—or, worse, unheeded.

Sam was sitting on the couch in his living room with bits of paper strewn around her.

'I had to get the CF thing straight in my head and you know what? Even if we're both carriers there's only a one in four chance of our child having CF. Those are pretty good odds, don't you think?'

'Weren't you the one who was saying we wouldn't bother with it until we got the test results?' he teased, although his heart had leapt at Sam's use of the word 'our'.

So he moved closer, stepping cautiously through the mess of paper, to take her hands and haul her to her feet, where he wrapped his arms around her and held her until he felt her body relax against his—slumping in tiredness from her emotional research.

'Come to bed,' he said, and when she began to object, he kissed the words away.

'We don't know anything yet,' he reminded her as he slid kisses down her neck. 'So, just for now...' he added, as his kisses reached the top of her breast, his lips seeking a way in beneath the loose tank top she was wearing.

Now his tongue had reached her nipple, lapped at it, and he felt her quiver, her body pressing closer to his, her lips now against his neck, her fingers tugging at the buttons on his shirt. Now she hauled his head, lips found lips, while their hands took over stripping their clothes off, and as his tongue met hers, felt it slide against his, desire ramped up a notch, and together they fell to the couch, his feet still entangled in his trousers, but nothing mattered but the sensation—the slide of skin on skin, fingers and lips teasing each other, the pressure for release building and building.

His fingers felt her heat and moistness, and her cry of, 'Please, Andy,' broke any restraint he'd managed to hold onto and he slid into her, moving with her, holding her arching body close, until with another cry she went limp in his arms and his own release surged through him, a groan of utter abandonment escaping him.

They lay, bodies slick with sweat, held together by the force of the passion they'd shared, neither moving, neither speaking, their breathing somehow synchronised. Until, after what seemed like for ever, Andy slid his body beneath hers, kicking off his trousers in the process, and looked up into her face.

'Repeat after me: I will forget about everything genetic until I get the test results.'

Sam smiled down at him, hair beautifully

tousled around her flushed face, eyes shining with the aftermath of sex.

'Consider it said,' she answered huskily. 'I'm far too pooped to think of anything tonight and should be back to my normal sensible self by morning.'

'Stay the night with me?' he asked, not wanting to let her go.

Ever!

But that was a way off yet.

He saw her smile and a sleepy nod, which was more than enough encouragement to slide off the couch and lift her in his arms, carrying her through to the bedroom, where he dropped her on the bed.

Sam looked up at him. She was so tired—pleasantly tired, ready to sleep tired—and yet she wanted more—something more—and as she turned onto her side, already half-asleep, she was aware of Andy pulling a sheet over her naked body, and knew what she'd wanted from him.

Love.

CHAPTER TEN

SAM WOKE TO find Andy gone—sometime in the night, she rather thought, vaguely recalling a phone ringing and Andy's hushed voice.

She stretched luxuriously in the big bed, aware of the musky smell of sex on her body, and pleasantly surprised to find memories of Andy's touch still alive on her nerve endings.

But noises outside the bedroom suggested he was back, his voice calling to her, 'Up, lazybones, breakfast in fifteen minutes!'

She leapt out of bed, heading for the shower, sorry she hadn't kept some clothes—undies at least—in Andy's bedroom. But once showered and clean, she pulled on the previous day's tank top and skirt.

Breakfast was a plate of bacon and eggs with hot rolls and butter, served on the balcony. What could be a better follow-up to a night of passion? The honey pot was on the table, already attracting the interest of flying insects, and a couple of small jars of jam the insects seemed equally interested in.

She sat, at peace with the world for the moment, until the smell of the bacon had her stomach roiling, and she fled to the bathroom.

'Dry toast?' Andy suggested sympathetically, as she came out.

She nodded.

'Well, go back out onto the balcony— I've removed the other breakfast but left the honey in case you needed something sweet.'

The brisk breeze from the ocean and, Sam suspected, a little air freshener had removed the smell of bacon and she was able to relax into a chair—but only for as long as it took to remember she had to make an appointment with a doctor to get her CF test results later today.

'We haven't talked about what happens if the test is positive,' Sam said, as the thought of finding out was already churning her delicate stomach.

'Because there's no point,' Andy said firmly. 'We could talk—discuss—for hours all the what-ifs, but why waste our breath on that? We'll wait and see then talk about what next, okay, love?'

There was the word again, the word that let hope creep into her heart.

He came and stood behind her, his hand resting on her shoulder, kneading gently, his fingers straying into her hair, lifting tendrils of it and letting them drop, running strands through his fingers...

He sighed and his fingers tugged gently at her hair so she lifted her face to look at him, look into eyes that didn't hide the confusion—despair?—he was feeling.

'I'd already decided—after Annabel—that it was best I didn't marry, didn't father children. Now here we are, and everything is different, Sam. And, anyway, I have to get back to work.'

He bent and kissed her on the lips—making her glad she'd put a bit of toothpaste on her finger and given herself a bit of a tooth clean so at least her breath was sweet.

But what use was that?

And why the kiss?

Hadn't he just told her he didn't want to marry?

But if he loved her...

There it was again—love.

Her mind was going round in circles, so she cleaned up the few dishes she'd used, stacked them in the dishwasher, and headed downstairs. What she needed was a swim to clear her head, keep busy so she didn't have to think about Andy, and the decision he'd made well before she'd happened along—his decision not to marry...

Andy couldn't remember a day at work when his mind hadn't been fully focussed on the job. Over the years he'd learned that even a slight distraction might mean he'd miss a minor change in a patient's status or, worse, forget a test he could have performed to get a better result.

So, to have his mind wandering to Sam, to the feel of her in his arms last night, the sweet musky smell of her, and most frequently of all to the test results she'd get today, was a new distraction.

He'd had enough distractions in the past to know how to retrieve his focus, but keeping it there?

Would she know by now?

His gut twisted at the thought, although he knew the percentages of her *not* being a carrier were far higher than a positive test.

Work—think about work!

But he'd held her in his arms as they'd slept, learned the way her body fitted best into his, and felt her heartbeat against his chest. And had known he loved her...

'Are you sure?' Sam demanded of the doctor, although such a question would have irritated her no end if she'd been working.

The doctor smiled and passed her the second sheet of paper.

'See, they've even sent us pictures!'

He pointed to two strings of figures printed on the page.

'This is the little bugger we want to look at.'

It was typed in red so it was totally obvious.

'See, no mutation in it whatsoever—check for yourself.'

She looked at the two sets of numbers and letters, which were both identical.

Her relief must have shown in her face for the doctor raised an eyebrow.

'Especially good news?' he said, and Sam smiled and nodded at him.

'Very, especially good,' she said, taking the papers from his hand and collecting her little backpack from the floor beside her chair.

'I'm glad,' the doctor told her. 'All the best to you.'

Sam departed, aware she should have been asking questions about the possibility of being one of the rare genetic carriers who didn't show up on tests, or discussing possible referrals to an obstetrician for the foetal test, but she'd sort all that out later. Right now she needed to send a text to Andy.

But that thought stopped her dead on the pavement outside the medical centre. She had absolutely no idea how Andy felt about her pregnancy.

She clutched her hand to her belly, protective of the new life there. There was still the foetal testing to be done but she felt reasonably certain that would be okay.

No! This baby was here to stay, with or without Andy.

With or without Andy?

The joyous bounce in her step slowed—stopped.

Just because *she* was desperate for a family it didn't mean Andy was.

And even if he did want one, did he want one with her?

There'd been no word of love between them—oh, he'd called her 'love'—but in the same way he might have called her 'sweetheart'.

But neither had she mentioned how she felt about him.

Too wary of rejection to lay her feelings bare?

Although early on she really hadn't been sure of love herself, hadn't been sure it wasn't just an overwhelming relief to have someone she knew and liked working with her.

Then slowly he'd crept into her thoughts—worse, into her blood, and bones, and sinews—until a casual touch could send her heart racing, a smile make her whole body sing.

Damn it all, life wasn't meant to be so complicated—she was sure of this. For the past three years she'd lived, if not at first but much more lately, quite happily single, never thinking about a long-term relationship, still living with a doubt that marriage to Nick had been *her* failure rather than his.

And *never* thinking about love...

'So, when should we get married?' Andy asked, walking into his flat where she'd been preparing a meal and handing her a large bunch of blue cornflowers. 'Must have had mainly girls arrive today to have had only blue ones at the hospital florist,' he added with a smile, then he kissed her cheek, and said, 'Well?'

Disturbed in ways she couldn't put in words, Sam thrust the flowers back at him.

'It's your flat—you'll know where you keep vases, if you have such things, and when did marriage come into the equation?'

'But of course, we'll get married. I want to be part of this child's life and isn't marriage the easiest way to achieve that? This is just the start—we can have a family!'

Sam closed the oven door on the chicken and lentil casserole she was making and turned to face him.

'There's more to marriage than having kids,' she said quietly.

'Of course, there is,' Andy said, the bunch of flowers still clutched in his hand. 'There's sharing lives, and hopes, and dreams, and ups and downs, I guess, and being there for each other through good times and bad, and just, well, having each other to lean on.'

Sam sighed. Should she prompt him? Tell him how she felt?

But if he didn't love her back, they'd both be embarrassed...

Embarrassed? She'd be downright devastated!

Damn it all, surely, she was old enough now to talk honestly about emotions and not get herself twisted up in knots like a fifteen-year-old.

Well, here goes nothing!

She took a deep breath, looked directly at him, aware there'd be challenge in her eyes.

'And love, Andy? Where does love come into it?'

He stared at her for a moment, then crossed the kitchen, rooting around in a cupboard and finally coming up with a large jar that had presumably held preserved fruit at some time.

He rinsed it then filled it with water, plonking the stems of the flowers into it.

Sam curbed the urge to say he should have trimmed the stalks and cut the string around them, she was far too tense.

Hands free now, he came towards her, put his hands on her shoulders and studied her face, his own concerned—a little wary.

'Sam,' he eventually said, 'I have loved you from the moment I first saw you in that bar. You married Nick, and I was happy for you both, but it didn't stop how I felt, so I kept away. And now you're here, lovelier than ever, carrying my child, and I've still been too…cowardly, I suppose, to tell you how I feel.'

He drew her closer, still speaking.

'You asked the question, Sam—the love question—the one I haven't dared ask you in case you weren't ready to love again, might never want to love again. But *my* love, if you'll accept it, is big enough for both of us.'

Now she was held against his chest, his arms tight around her, her face buried in the curve of his neck.

'You never said,' she muttered against his shirt.

'Cowardly, I know, but to have spoken of it, and been rejected, would have been almost more than I could bear.'

She moved so she could hold him, tightened her arms, and still talking into his shirt muttered, 'Rejected? Never! Of course I love you! How could I not?'

She leaned back so she could see his face, the smile quirking up one side of his lips.

'You are the kindest, most unselfish man I've ever met. You'd do anything you could to help others—everyone can see that from your doctoring. But you're warm, and protective, and, well, you're Andy, and I love you with all my heart!'

It was some time later that Sam found the words she needed, to ask one final, vital question.

One that she hardly dared to ask...

'Would you have walked away from a relationship if I'd been a carrier?'

He looked at her and shook his head.

'I doubt very much that I could have, Sam, not loving you as much as I do. But we'd have had to have had a serious conversation about children and, knowing you want them so much, that might have made things different.'

There was a pause that made her heart stand still.

'*You* might have walked away!' he added.

She moved back into his arms, holding him tightly.

'I couldn't walk away from you, Andy. I love you more than life itself, so you're stuck with me.'

She eased back so she could lay a palm against his cheek.

'And given that I could still be one of the

five percent who don't show up as carriers, we'll have this baby, and any other baby, tested, okay?'

And, again, he drew her close.

'I like the sound of other babies,' he murmured, then kissed her on the lips, a kiss that said so much that could never be put into words. A kiss that was a promise and a pledge and a deep declaration of love…love that would last for ever.

EPILOGUE

THEY WERE MARRIED three weeks later, high
on the cliff, beneath the lighthouse. With
the sparkling sea as a backdrop, innumera-
ble members of Andy's family—who'd been
waiting a long time to see this spectacle—
and Sam's mother, flown out from the clinic
on the Cambodian border, as guests, the two
of them repeated their vows, eyes on each
other, everyone else melting away.

'I love you,' Andy said as he bent to kiss
her lips.

'And I you,' she said on a breath before
those lips met hers.

But as they walked into the lighthouse restaurant, she was met by a crowd of men and
women, friends from her past, some she'd
kept in sporadic touch with and others she'd
thought lost for ever.

Andy had found every one of them and

had organised for them to come and share their special day.

And suddenly she was home again, among the friends she'd fled three years ago, and home had become a safe haven, a real home, with Andy by her side for ever.

* * * * *

If you enjoyed this story, check out these other great reads from Meredith Webber

Conveniently Wed in Paradise
The Doctors' Christmas Reunion
A Wife for the Surgeon Sheikh
New Year Wedding for the Crown Prince

All available now!